What most readers don't understand is that authors thrive best where people leave deserving reviews, or pass on the feeling that remains with them after they finish the book. Beside telling all your friends about it, please, if you can spare the time, leave a review of **Firelight on Dark Water** wherever you purchased it from.
Thank you

Cybermouse Books

Copyrights;

Cybermouse MultiMedia Ltd.,
101 Cross Lane
Sheffield S10 1WN

www.cybermouse-multimedia.com

First published by Cybermouse Books 2015

In the design of this book, Cybermouse Multimedia Ltd. have
made every effort to avoid infringement of any established copyright.
If anyone has valid concern re any unintended infringement please contact
us first at the above address.

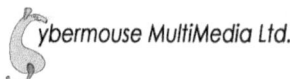

Firelight
on
Dark Water

A Celebration of the

Warm and Wonderful

from the imagination of

Bill Allerton

In the writing of these stories I have accompanied my imagination to strange and wonderful places. Some of them are accessibly down-to-earth, but others are populated by people even stranger than myself.

Because it is acknowledged that all tales, whether novels, poems or short fiction, are simple ideas sifted through a filter of the writer's own life experience and subliminal wishes, this must then be my unique interpretation of all the people and places that exist on Planet Bill.

Good grief.

What a weird world I must be.

Bill

This book is dedicated to

William James and Edward Lewis
Allerton

Who arrived Bright & Beautiful
On the morning of
26th. November 2015

Firelight on Dark Water;

'I am very jealous of your skill with dialogue. The economy of it and the precise way you catch all kinds of talk from all sorts of people...

I love the way things and people recur in the book; but I love the range and the surprises too...

I like the 'you' who emerges from these stories, with this alertness to language and a sense of the odd...

I think the stories are kind, while dealing with loneliness and death and loss and madness and funny love and time and all the mess that usually gets people to be unkind...

Your short stories tease me to keep going back...'

Rony Robinson, Sony Award-winning BBC Radio presenter and Playwright

The Fox & The Fish;

'the writing is so original and the dialogue so inventive and funny it cracks me up. It's brilliant, clever and lyrical. You have one hell of a talent...'

Clem Cairns, Fish Publishing, organiser of the international 'Fish Prize'

Contents:

Appendix: Other Titles in the Cybermouse Books range

The Comer

Many, many years ago, when I was an apprentice, I worked for a man who, later in my life, became one of my dearest friends and colleagues. His name was Wilf. And he was a 'character' in the real spirit of the term. The sayings in the story are his and I'm sorry that I can't remember more of them at this time. One of his sayings, he was a keen gardener, was that you should always let your worst enemy prune your roses. By cutting them back to a minimum that was hard to condone while doing it yourself, you were guaranteed a bumper crop the following year.

The same rule applies to writing, whether it be a poem, short fiction or a novel. Outside influence and opinion should be sought and welcomed. It only makes you better.

Wilf taught me many other things when, after he retired, he came to work for me. Not the least was the ability to take it on the chin and keep smiling.

The following story is true, almost, but is a true reflection of the lovely man he was.

The Comer

Oh! Hello.

Come on in.

Sorry, I didn't hear you at the door. Been there long? Oh, right. I was upstairs. Can't hear a thing with the hoover on. Haven't seen you for a while. You all right? Good. Well, it gets a bit quiet these days, but I'm all right. Yes. Here, let me take your coat. You're sure? It's no trouble. Alright. Let me put the fire on then. That's better. It'll warm up in a minute. Cup of coffee?

Good!

Oh, Wilf? Yes, I know. It's sad, but if you've gotta go, then that's the way to do it. Is it really? That long? Yes. Before you know it, almost. Do you know, I remember when summers used to last forever…

He was sat in his chair the last time I saw him. Oh, sorry! Will you sit down? Let me get that kettle on. Won't be a minute. Put your feet up on the hearth, it's warmer.

There's some chocolate on the mantel, help yourself. Oh, go on, nobody's looking. I've a cake here that Mary left, too. Seems a shame. Too much just for one. I know you'll help me. Oh stop it, it won't hurt for once.

Sat there large as life he was. Can see him now. Did look well, but then he always did. Here, let me put that paper under it. It'll be alright then. Won't mark the table. Hattie really looked after him, you know. Yes. Worshipped him. Could be a bugger though.

Did you like the chocolate? Have some more with your coffee. Wilf always did that. Always had a bar of chocolate on the mantel. Said he saved it there for when I dropped in. Said he knew I liked a piece of chocolate. Never quite the same since Hattie went. Two years? Four! It's like I said. Before you know it almost. I remember the sun was shining. No, the last time I saw *him* I mean.

I used to call regular. Saturday mornings mostly. Sometimes during the week if I needed somewhere to run to for half an hour. He'd always put the kettle on and there was always a piece of chocolate on the end of the mantel. Didn't have to ask after a while. He'd just smile and say 'Get on with it. Help yourself. Nobody's looking.'

A bit more cake? You've soon polished that off. Hang on, there's plenty in the tin. I always wash it out before she calls for it. Keeps bringing it back with another in. Do they still make these biscuits? Probably call them something else now. Something 'trendy'. I remember it was sunny because it shone in through the window and in through the holes in his cardie and he had that pale green shirt on and he hadn't had a shave for days. He still had some colour in his hair you know, even at that age. I remember it was sticking up at the back like Alfalfa.

Would you like some more milk in that? No? Alright. It's not the same now is it? The bottled stuff tastes like plastic and the cartons taste of wax. Here, let me take that plate. Bit more cake? You can manage a little bit. Oh, go on, nobody's looking. There I go again. That's one of Wilf's. He had one or two like that. When someone wouldn't pay he'd say they needed *a stiff letter from Fernoughety,* or he'd say, *How many F's in bugger?* Or if he couldn't get to the bottom of someone, he'd say they wanted *'mesmerising by the public anarchist'.* He *was* a lad.

I've got some beef in the fridge. Too much for me. I'm going to make a sandwich in a minute. There's some pickles on the cellar. Can't buy just enough beef for one these days. *And* it shrivels up to nowt when you cook it. Don't know what they do to it. And by the time I've had half of it I'm fed up and me teeth are tired. Do me a favour really. You will? Oh, good. I'll get the plates out.

His trousers were all shiny on the tops of his legs, I remember that. And he was always so clean when Hattie was here. He didn't smell though, say what you like, he was clean that way. And I remember one clip was undone on his braces and I was sat there listening to him talking; he could talk you know, lovely man, learnt a lot just by listening to him, things I could never buy, like attitudes and how to tell what a person was thinking, just by reading the little signs, like, how they sat, and even how they ate their chocolate. Took it all with him, except for what he taught me and I'll never forget that. Do you want some Branston? Mustard? I think there's a pickled onion left from Christmas. No? Well, they keep, don't they.

Well, I was sat with my feet up on the hearth and I caught sight of something move on the chairs where they'd been pushed under the table. 'Wilf!' I said, 'There's something under the table! By God it's a cat! A cat's got in, Wilf!' He just smiled and reached under the table and lifted out this beautiful grey, black and white cat and sat it on his lap. The cat curled up right away and closed its eyes. You sort of wanted to do that around Wilf. You always felt safe somehow. Here, the tea's mashed, let me rinse that out. Two sugars? Oh? Slimming, are we? Well, nobody's looking here. Anyway this cat's sat there purring and I could see its fur trembling away like a kettle on the hob and I said 'Whose's the cat Wilf?'

'It's a Comer,' he said. A *what* I said? ' A Comer,' he says, 'Comes and goes when it pleases. It always knows where to come when it's hungry though. Stands there meeowing at the door to be let in. Turns its nose up at everything at first, then when it thinks nobody's looking, it eats everything in sight. It's a wonder it leaves the plate.'

'Whose is it then?' I said. 'Don't know,' he said, 'I think the neighbour feeds it as well. Wherever it comes from it's well looked after, just look at its fur. You can see somebody loves it. It's a nice cat.'

'How long's it been around?' I said. 'Oh,' he says, 'A month or two. It doesn't seem to want to go home much. It's always here or out in the back.'

Well, I leaned across to stroke it and under the fur there's this collar.

'Hey Wilf,' I said, 'It's got a collar on, look.'

'Oh aye,' he says.

I turned the collar around and out from under all the fur comes this round disc.

Another slice? Good! The bread usually ends up stale before I get round to eating it all. Some more tea? The kettle's still warm. Won't take a minute. Sorry? Oh, the disc. It said *Harry*. I said, 'Is that it then, Wilf? The cat's name's *Harry*?' He just sat there stroking it.

'Suppose so,' he said, 'If that's what it says. Don't really know. Doesn't matter. It comes and goes when it pleases. Except when it's hungry. What's in a name, eh puss?'

When I turned the disc over it said, Wilf Sargeant, 39 Peregrine Rd.

I said 'It's yours, Wilf! Somebody must have bought it for you to keep you company. I'm glad. It looks a nice cat.'

'Don't really know,' he said, 'It just turned up one day and I fed it and it just keeps coming back. I told you, it's a Comer.'

Here, let me put those in the sink. You've got to go? Well, take the chocolate with you. Eat it when nobody's looking. Oh, It's all gone. Never mind. I can get some more. You know, I think I knew then that he wasn't far away. You get this feeling about people, don't you? It's in the way they hold their head and in the things they say. It sort of signals where they are down that road and how far they've got to go before they reach the end and then, would you believe it, a few days later and he's gone. Oh, sorry, of course, you didn't take your coat off did you. You weren't stopping. It looks a nice coat. Hope it keeps the rain off.

You'll come again? Yes, anytime. It doesn't matter. I'm always here. Oh, yes… sorry. I'll listen out for you next time.

Yes, I promise.

And you.

Bye.

Meeeoow!

Alright, you can come on out now. Nobody's looking. And it's no good hiding under the table, I know where you are. There might be a bit of beef left? No? Well, they've eaten all the chocolate. Now don't look at me like that or you'll get the pickle. I'm only kidding. There's some more on the cellar.

We'll put another bar out on the mantel. Seems a bit quiet now, but they'll be back, won't they?

We know a comer when we see one, *don't we* Harry?

The Rocket Home

Some events stick in your memory in a way that allows you to take them out, shake off the dust and relive the excitement, despite the fact that some of them have uncomfortable elements that sit as irritating as a burr under your saddle.

The main incident here happened so quickly that it has an almost dream-like quality in my memory. That it is true, I am certain, although some of the rationalisation may be the result of an adult mind analysing the actions of itself at an earlier age.

What I can't deny, however, is how wrong it felt to be moved, and that the blame I heaped upon myself, that was then heaped upon by others, still bears a weight.

The Rocket Home

Grandpa drove his motorbike home in the October rain. It boomed along the passage and stood rattling the yard until the shed doors creaked shut and the keys jangled and he eased himself into the kitchen, bringing with him the smell of beer from the dray and the taste and wet of outside. I earned a tea-time penny, pulling his overall legs over his boots and rolling them up under his chair.

We sat in tiny corners in the tiniest of kitchens to watch each other, and Grandpa in particular, as he bent over his plate to see what was for tea. And we wondered if this time the beer and the cold would get the better of him again, and if he'd slowly close his eyes and fall forwards, smiling quietly into the potatoes and rabbit gravy.

This night, he must have been too cold. He asked Grandma to bank up the fire. She threw a few last lumps of coal onto an already roaring fire and then the slack from the bottom of the scuttle. It hit the flames with a whoosh and a ball of orange flame disappeared up the chimney. As we watched him, Grandpa settled down to eat.

Slowly, in fact so slowly that at first we might not have noticed, we found ourselves being drawn towards the fireplace. The letterbox began to flap a metal tattoo against the back door. The air ripped around the edges of the frame. We bent as though a strong wind were taking us into the grate and hearth.

First Grandma, then Grandpa, then Mom, then Dad. They all bent towards the fire to stare up the chimney above the Yorkshire. There began a deep moaning. It grew into a roar like Grandpa's motorbike, then louder, until it shook the air in the room. Suddenly, everyone began to shout and move around me.

'The chimney's on fire, you daft old bugger,' Grandpa said.

'It wasn't me that come in late and drunk,' Grandma said.

Mom said, 'Shut up the pair of you.'

Dad said, 'You're both daft old buggers. Throw some salt on it!'

'I'm going to Simpson's,' Mom said, and shot off to the shop next-door-but-one to see if they would be so kind, and she knew there was a public phone three-hundred yards away at the other end of the street, but would they mind ringing the fire brigade as our house was on fire.

I was half in, half out of the back door getting underfoot when Dad threw a big handful of salt up the chimney.

Whoosh, it went, with a white fizz and a sizzling sound and Dad jumped back across the kitchen as a hot white cloud followed him from the hearth.

'It didn't work,' he croaked, then, 'Billy, bugger off in the yard and stay there!'

All this time the roar was getting louder and louder until it played a note like a deep church organ and the darkening air came whistling in through the open door and the paper was curling on the table, the edges of the pages lifting and rolling towards the hearth and the dust from the rug was flying and the air filled with sounds that fixed your body right through like a spike.

I stood there watching this thing that was happening to somebody somewhere else and the voices sounded different and distant and Grandpa said, 'I'll throw water on the fire.' and Dad said 'NO!', but he was too late.

The kitchen filled with steam and from inside the chimney there came an explosion like thunder and the roar grew louder and deeper. Dad kicked me on his way out and bundled me through the door into the yard.

We stood out there in the growing dark and watched the flames shame the moon as they leapt from the chimney. It seemed to rock with a power and to jump against the blue of the clearing late evening sky. It spewed sparks and soot and great billowing clouds of writhing smoke at all our attempts to stop it. The flames grew longer and sharper and the air whistled around our feet and into the back door to come out again, scarred, twisted and angry with flame, from the top of the chimney.

Looking back and, being me, it felt as if it had been a rocket that had hurtled earthwards from another place, and I had been brought along inside it. I felt the earth begin to turn under my feet and thought I saw the stars move as the rocket pushed and pushed against the ground, spinning us around so that we would forget where we had come from just a few short days ago. A place down the street with a small garden, and kindnesses, and whitewash, and flowers.

The fire brigade arrived with ringing bells and ladders and a pat on the head and I wanted to tell them where I was from but I couldn't say it. I wanted to tell them that I wasn't from here, but from somewhere before here. Before an argument about me sent us packing up the street from Nan's. Before this night set my imagination on fire and filled it with dreams of taking another rocket home. If I was ever that lucky.

The hose they pushed in the chimney poured soot and water down into the kitchen and from the back door there came the sound of bricks falling inside a long, dark tunnel.

The ladders came down and went away leaving water and silence behind them inside the cracked concrete bell of the yard. I watched steam curl star-wards from the quiet chimney.

I heard the bricks chink and tick in their cooling and the lights coming back on in the kitchen after the fuse was fixed, and realised that we had settled here, and that I had to make the best of that in a new world where the land was only cobble and concrete and nothing ever grew except the weeds in the crack between the house and the pavement and the leaves on the way-up trees behind the high wall, where night-felled birds watched and whispered about us, nattering with quiet clicks and whistles, wondering if we would still be here in the morning or would we too have flown off.

I stood in the yard on bare concrete, perhaps for the first time fully aware of both my feet. I lifted them and set them down again firmly on this new planet of my life.

But the night remained. It wrapped itself around me with a cloak of smoke and steam and soot and the fear and frailty of older people, and visions of warm attic beds with sheets that tasted of tears and scorch until they'd all been washed next day and planted like flags into the new landscape of the yard, so that the silent, watching birds would know that I had arrived.

Circles in the Frost

For many years I was a member of Heeley Writers in Sheffield. Between us we produced a yearly magazine of an unusually high quality and overall the experience was a blessed influence on my own work. We were a diverse group, some authors for children, published or un-, novelists, me, and a couple of article writers and 'faction' authors, one of whom is trotted out on TV each time there's a UFO needs explaining.

For many years we were a happy bunch until, as many of you may have found in such organisations, the group dynamic changed.

Change can be a good thing, but this one wasn't. It killed the group and this little note is my way of saying R.I.P to the good times we had. One good thing that the group gave us was the ability to challenge each other and ourselves. The following story was written in response to just such a challenge. The aim was to explore 'envy', and the way that emotion could lock you down into a pattern of life… so…

Ever envied something a close friend or relative has? Her way with boys… her dress sense… her appetite that never gains her any excess pounds no matter what… even her father?

In this story of youth, shared family and football support, two teenage girls circle each other and their relationships… each envying the other their instinctive traits… until love brings them both full-circle.

Circles in the Frost

'What time is it?'

Shirley rummaged amongst the cuffs of her neatly pressed blouse for the watch she had forgotten in her haste. She could see it now, ticking away to itself on the staff toilet window sill. She hoped it would still be there on Monday. She rubbed an itch on the end of her nose. Her hands smelled of clean leather beneath the fragrance of soap.

'Half-past four,' said Glenys, withdrawing into her duffel coat. She looked at the tops of her new shoes and bit down hard on her disappointment.

'He'll be here soon,' said Shirley, looking round the corner for her boyfriend. She twisted a few blonde strands between the fingers of her left hand, her purse clutched tightly in the other.

'It doesn't matter,' Glenys's voice lifted no higher than her fading hopes.

'I'm sorry,' said Shirley, which wasn't much comfort, but Saturday afternoons off were rare, and she had done her best.

'It really doesn't matter!' Glenys was still pretending to admire the foyer lights reflected in the black patent slingbacks. Shirley had brought them across for her last night. Special, for today.

Glenys heard the rattle of loose change that was Norman's habit, and looked up.

'I'll be going then,' said Shirley, stepping backwards to link arms with Norman.

I'd settle for him, thought Glenys.

His hand had been warm and dry when he'd patted her cheek at the bonfire. Right now she would have settled for anything except this incredible falling sensation of being stood up. She looked up at Norman and imagined being stroked instead of patted, and not just her cheek either.

'Whatever you want!' she replied. The wasted time caught in her throat and threatened to choke her, 'I'm sorry Shirl, I didn't mean to snap.'

Shirley unwrapped herself from Norman and hugged Glenys briefly.

'Wait till I see him on Monday. New under-manager or not, he'll get the length of my tongue!'

Norman stepped up to Glenys, smoothed the hood of her duffel with one hand and patted her cheek in quiet embarrassment.

'See you, Kiddo.'

His hand carried the bitter tang of copper coins, but now, away from the scent of the bonfire, the rest of him smelled animal and warm. His palm was still dry.

'Never mind love,' said Shirley, retrieving Norman, 'We'll walk you to the bus stop.'

'No, no, you mustn't. Norman's got the tickets now and if you don't hurry up you'll miss the cartoon. I'll be alright, it's still early.'

'Okay,' said Shirley, glad to be freed from the responsibility she always felt for Glenys, 'Don't talk to any strange men.'

Glenys smiled. She watched as Shirley clattered and Norman jingled up the steps into the Pictures.

If my hand was in his pocket, she thought, *It wouldn't be his change I'd be rattling.*

She jinked across the busy afternoon street and walked down the gennel to the bus stop. Leaning against the shelter was a skinny youth in tight black jeans and a leather jacket. His hair was fanned into a crest of peacock blues and magentas that gave him a curiously symmetrical appearance. In his nose was a gold ring that broke the illusion. On the back of his jacket, in lurid letters like dripping wet blood, it said,

'The Cure'

Hmm, thought Glenys, *I'm not convinced it's working.*

She remembered Shirley's last words, and kept three good paces away. The youth smiled at her and she shivered.

The bus arrived and Glenys let him board first. As he went inside he half turned to see if she was following him, only to see her nip upstairs to sit with the chokers on the top deck.

By the look of him, she'd thought, *I'd sooner have a good cough.*

The Poly was just down the road from the shoe shop where Shirley worked. She lunched there, subsidised, thanks to Glenys's pass. They tried to meet every day but if lectures ran over then Glenys was late. She felt guilty, but couldn't think why. Shirley just found another man to talk to.

This Monday she was early and sat down at an empty table with her back to the aisle. Shirley sneaked up and skipped a tray off the back of her head.

'Hi Kiddo, Happy Monday!'

'Hi Shirley', said Glenys, without looking round, 'Happy Monday yourself, see how you like it.'

Shirley returned to the table, her tray brimming with the thickest, fattest, sweetest things the canteen could devise.

Glenys looked on, wistful, but no longer surprised as the cottage cheese and crackers found its way unerringly to her hips.

The conversation fell into brief silences with rapid-fire from Shirley between courses.

'Derek says he did turn up. Stood across the road by the top of the gennel 'cause he wasn't sure if I was having him on or not. Didn't want me and my friends, *pass the sauce Glen,* hanging round a street corner somewhere laughing at him. *The pie's nice.* Swears blind he didn't see me, asked what I was wearing so I told him.'

'Oh', he says, '...that *were* you then. I didn't recognize you with your smock off!'

'You should be so lucky! I said. *Do you want that cracker?*'

'Your hair was all shook out and wiggly,' he said, 'Do you mind,' I said, '*Oh, thanks Glen.* Cost me all of three quid to have that styled.'

'Anyway,' he says, 'I bet you had me fixed up with some right old boiler.'

'Here,' I said, 'She's a very nice girl.'

'Yeah, for a boiler,' he said, 'I bet that's always been her trouble. Bet she weren't a patch on that little cracker I saw getting on the bus. Well, I nearly poured shoe cream down his suit trousers. Would have served him right too. What's up with you girl?'

Glenys sat there open mouthed.

'Glen?'

Shirley was fighting hard to forego a mouthful of banana and double cream until Glenys replied. She lost.

On Wednesday nights, Shirley met Glenys for coffee in the little cafe below the North Stand. The single room with its red and black Formica counter was dominated by an ancient boiler. The chrome had long since rubbed off and the copper and brass were now plated with condensation and tannin.

The stools were high and spindly, and Shirley's legs wrapped easily around them. Glenys kept trying to get two feet onto one rail and gave the impression that a fall was imminent. Her Doc Martens didn't help.

She had been at college all day and most of the evening. She was tired. She caught sight of herself in the mirror behind the counter. Her pale brown hair was as lank as the pies in the cabinet.

'And who's going to unravel *my* Clingfilm,' she wondered.

The walls of the caff were covered with fixture lists from the Third Division, except for the corner where the toaster had flared one Saturday lunchtime. The scorch marks were almost hidden by a poster of a matador, killing a bull that would have kept the place in corned beef sandwiches for a year.

Shirley was wittering on about nothing much and Glenys sat savouring the magic names that had been roared overhead. Li-ver-pool, Li-ver-pool. Ghosts from her twelfth year. Wens-dy, Wens-dy.

That was when her father had died. Suddenly. Without warning.

Uncle Bob had taken her and Shirley to all the home games he could manage, just like when dad was alive. Before then they had taken it in turns to shepherd the two chattering red and white imps between the turnstiles and the police horse's legs.

For one fleeting moment she was back on the terrace, her dad's gabardine wrapped around her shoulders against the drizzle, her feet tap-tapping in the cold and her face an open wound of support.

Then it was gone.

Shirley was still wittering.

'…following Norman up the path and I said, 'Hey, hang on a minute, I can't keep up in these heels. 'Then take 'em off you daft bugger', he said.'

'Hey,' I said, 'Mind your language in front of a lady,' and he looks round and says, 'I can't see your Glenys anywhere! And she wouldn't wear four inch heels to go for a walk in the park.' Well, I could have smacked him right there, except he's right.'

Glenys couldn't look at the poster of the bull with the sword through its neck without thinking of Norman and Shirley.

'You goad people Shirl, you really do. For the last three weeks all he's had from you is how clever Derek is and how much brighter he's made the shop and, to cap it all, you even get to work on time. That's as likely as these clowns,' she jerked her thumb at the ceiling, '…ever getting back into the First Division.'

Shirley watched her coffee cooling as she spooned the knickerbocker glory into a pursing mouth. She knew Glen was right, but men were only things, with urges. It wasn't that she minded the urges, she had some of her own, but did they have to approach her 'urge first'?

She looked over the loft of her breasts and wondered what it was like to be able to see the tops of your thighs while you were sat on a chair. Glenys would know, but she didn't like to ask her. One look at Shirley's chest and the men became a single hormone, with a smile like the Cheshire Cat.

With December came the damp, and long dark nights. The air was cold but far from crisp and Glenys walked through it as if she waded in marshmallow.

'Oh, come on Glen! The shops close in an hour.'

Glenys shuffled a little faster behind Shirley. Her arms were full of boxes and the carrier bag in her left hand was cutting slowly through her fingers. She wouldn't have minded so much if any of them had been hers.

'Don't look at me like that, Glen. You could have stayed at home.'

Glenys looked up at the coloured lights strung across the road. The bulbs steamed in the early evening mist that was turning gradually into drizzle.

'Fat chance!'

She stopped outside a large department store, 'Look Shirl, just how far down this list have we got?'

'I can't remember,' said Shirley, 'You've got it somewhere. I think it's in the Boots bag.'

'Is that the one trying to guillotine my elbow or the one that's severed two fingers off my left hand?'

'Oh, don't be so bloody dramatic,' said Shirley, 'Come on, we'll get a coffee in here… What are you still stood there for?'

'Oh. Sorry Shirl, but as you walked away the string slipped through the ring in my nose and for a minute I was lost.'

Shirley stomped off into the cafeteria with her nose high and her shoulders back. Two middle-aged men sucked in their stomachs and moved aside for safety.

'Find us a table, Glen,' she shouted, knowing that Glenys would be right behind her.

The two men smiled at Glenys. Life was safer now that Shirley had passed. Glenys watched their stomachs resume the customary hang over their trouser waistbands, and returned the smile grudgingly.

She picked one of the side tables, over against the wall. In the corner was an old lady, slumped inside a once-fashionable top coat with a large Astrakhan collar.

Three empty coffee cups patterned the white Formica with rings. The old girl was drifting in and out of sleep as Glenys watched. She piled all the parcels into the empty seat against the wall opposite the old dear, and sat next to them so they didn't spill out into the aisle. Shirley arrived with two lukewarm coffees and sat next to the old woman, glancing at her suspiciously.

'It's alright,' said Glenys, 'She won't bite.'

' Shhh,' said Shirley, 'Don't be so bloody rude!'

'What are you going to do, Shirl, when you're old like that,' Glenys nodded towards the old woman, '…and people think you keep pickled walnuts in your stockings… and nobody gets out of the way of your chest any more, eh?'

Shirley squirmed in embarrassment. Her face was red over the coffee cup, her eyes darting sideways.

'Glenys' she hissed, 'Are you daft?'

'No,' said Glenys, pointing, 'But she's deaf, and her hearing aid's fallen out.'

Shirley kicked her under the table. 'That's why I've got to do it now,' she said.

'Do what?' asked Glenys, flexing life back into her fingers.

'You know. Love, and that.'

'What's 'that',' asked Glenys, teasing.

'You know, men, and that.'

Despite her initial brashness, Shirley found herself becoming embarrassed. Her face flushed.

Glenys leaned across the table and caught one of her hands.

'Look, Shirl. You're only eighteen. You've got all your life…'

'I won't,' said Shirley with tight precision, 'Always be eighteen.'

The old lady in the corner stirred and began to snore quietly.

'You're afraid Shirl, aren't you? That's it, isn't it?'

Glenys pressed her fingers into Shirley's hand.

'Don't be. You got me, babe.'

Shirley's eyes filled with tears. She propped her head in her hands, and dripped salt rain into the coffee.

'Sorry, Glen,' she managed, through lips that were wet and trembling, her voice barely crossing the table, 'I've never told you, or anyone. I'm scared, and it's because of Uncle Fred.'

Glenys sat up sharply, 'Dad? What about my dad?' She felt the sting of tears behind her own eyes, 'I don't understand.'

'Don't you see,' Shirley wiped her nose on the back of her hand, then remembering where she had put her handbag, rummaged in it for a tissue.

'I go home every night and look at my dad, and then I see that picture where your dad's stood with him like two peas in a pod. Don't you see? They were twins. It could so easily have been him instead of Uncle Fred and that scares me to death.'

'Come on Shirl, lightning doesn't strike twice. Nothing wrong with your Dad's ticker.'

'You still don't see!' Shirley's eyes welled again after the outburst, like storm drains after sudden summer thunder. She sobbed quietly for a moment, her breath racked unevenly.

This time, quieter, almost to herself,

'You still don't see.'

'What I do see,' said Glenys, wearing a smile she hoped would be infectious, '…is that your mascara is halfway to your chin.'

'Stop it, Glen.' Shirley recovered slightly. A half-smile quivered her lips before giving up. 'My dad's the only one that loves me for me, and not just for, well, you know, and without him I'd die, or I might as well.'

'That's not true Shirl. There are hundreds of men out there that will fancy your... find you attractive... just for yourself. And even if it was,' said Glenys gently, 'You still got me, babe.'

The old lady in the corner smiled, her eyes closed, but missing nothing.

Shirley sniffed then cleared her throat.

'Thanks Glen, and you got me too.'

'Thanks,' said Glenys, not stopping to think how she meant that.

They arrived back at Connaught Terrace and Shirley fumbled with the door then flew through the rooms looking for her father, discarding her coat on the hall floor. Glenys stood there, hung like a Christmas tree with boxes, bags, presents, and couldn't move. Her left shoe was down the sleeve of Shirley's coat and her right one in the left hand pocket.

'Aunt Mavis?'

'Our Glenys! What are you playing at girl?'

'Double or Drop I think, Auntie. Give us a hand will you?'

Mavis took the parcels from her and stacked them on the first stair. Glenys untangled herself from the coat and hung it on the hook behind the door. She put her arm around Aunt Mavis and hugged her.

'Soon be nineteen,' said Mavis, returning the gentle pressure, 'My, and you're a bonny girl.'

'Thanks Auntie, parts of me are and parts of me aren't, but it seems they're all the wrong parts.'

'Away with you, our Glenys.' She tucked a stray lock of hair behind Glenys' ear and tapped lovingly on her forehead.

'You've words in here will melt the hardest heart and show it how to laugh. I'll tell you kid, make them laugh and they'll follow you like you were the Pied Piper.'

'Thanks Auntie.'

Glenys found Shirley in the kitchen, clinging like a leech to Uncle Bob.

'Hi Kiddo,' he said, pulling strands of Shirley's hair out of his mouth,

'What's up with *this* one today?'

He patted Shirley's behind affectionately.

'Oh, nothing much.'

Glenys was suddenly jealous. Try as she might she still couldn't look at Uncle Bob without feeling that she had just woken from a bad dream and it was alright because there was her Dad patting Shirley the way he always had.

'Nothing more than usual anyway.' She turned and walked back through the dining room into the hall.

Mavis caught her arm as she walked stiffly past. She recognized the look and pulled Glenys's coat to and fastened the top button.

'Coats don't keep out all the cold,' she said, 'No matter how tight we keep them fastened. Sometimes you have to let it in, and with your love and memories turn it into something warm and good, but a bit at a time, eh girl?'

Glenys found she couldn't speak. She nodded. Mavis kissed her forehead.

'Give my love to your Mam.'

Glenys still couldn't seem to get both feet on one rail. She had just given up when the cafe door clicked open, and cold December air condensed the steam above the boiler.

She put down her cup in surprise.

'Hello Norman, what are you doing here?'.

'Hi kid, Shirl can't make it.' Norman sat on the stool just below and to one side of the bull. Glenys didn't know whether to laugh or cry.

'Derek's asked her to work late, seeing as it's nearly Christmas.'

'And you got the job of running along to tell Glenys, eh?'

'Actually,' he said, 'It was my idea. Shirley said you'd be alright.'

'Well, thank you very much, Norman. It was good of you to think of me.'

Normans tongue stumbled.

'I, er, I do… sometimes.'

His eyes focused anywhere except on Glenys. With the lists behind her she felt like a fixture he'd missed and was now too embarrassed to ask if he could still play.

'Oh, that's good,' said Glenys, patting his knee. It was dry and warm, and the cloth was rougher than the palm of her hands. The sensation was far from unpleasant.

'I suppose you're going then, now you've done your duty?'

'No,' said Norman.

'So,' said Glenys, as she fumbled with the horn-shaped buttons of her coat, 'Am I to infer that this is a rare privilege, and that you are over eighteen and here of your own free will?'

Norman looked down at her.

'You say the strangest things, Glen.'

'Yeah, I do, don't I,' she said, opening the door for him.

Shirley tapped her feet impatiently. The arches were killing her but what the heels did for her legs was worth the agony. Derek was late. She'd twisted his arm mercilessly for this date. It was strange, he didn't seem to want to meet her outside work, yet all the male customers did. Shirley couldn't understand it. She'd wondered if he was married, or gay or something.

A bus pulled up across the road and a little way down from where Shirley stood. The people got off and separated without acknowledgement. She heard the muffled ting of a bell and the bus pulled away in a roar of dark fumes, taking its light and its warmth with it.

Suddenly, Shirley was living her worst nightmare. She stood alone at the corner of the park, away from the pooling streetlights. Her pony-tail twitched nervously across the collar of her sheepskin as she looked around for help.

There was none.

Across the road an outrageous figure stood at the bus stop, staring at her. Shirley could feel his eyes on hers. He stepped slowly to the edge of the pavement. Shirley's feet slid sideways, taking her two steps around the corner, but it was darker there. She slid back. The youth was still there, still looking. He looked down at his boots then stepped forward into the road, his eyes on Shirley's own white saucers. Shirley fled to the next gate, some fifty feet down the hedge and stopped, breathless. The youth now stood where, moments before, Shirley had been tapping her heels.

She moved away from the hedge to stand under a street lamp and search in her handbag for the metal tail-comb. The street was deserted, Corrie would be on the box, and this was all she had.

Her thoughts fled to Norman. She would make it up to him tomorrow. If there was a tomorrow.

The youth swung round the corner then started to walk slowly in her direction.

'Come and get it mate!' she thought violently, then suddenly found her feet had more sense than her anger, and took off up the road as fast as four inch heels would allow.

The youth padded softly after her, the Airwear soles springing and making light work of matching her pace.

Shirley found herself more repentant with every footstep, 'Dear God, if only… Oh dad, mom, please…'

Behind her the youth began to shout.

She slowed and pushed aside her panic to listen. A rapist wouldn't shout, would he?

'Shirley? Shirley?'

She stopped, 'Oh My God!'

The light glinted off the ring through his nose.

'Derek?'

It was Tuesday lunchtime and Glenys was late. Shirley had added another man to her collection. Glenys shook her head at him from behind Shirley's back. He got the message.

'What is it about you Glen?' asked Shirley, 'That's another one you've frightened away.'

'Don't worry about it Shirl. All the boys in here see me park my broomstick in a morning, and the black cat's a dead giveaway. As for the pointed hat…'

'Oh, shut up Glen,' said Shirley, swapping an empty dinner plate for the fruit salad and cream, 'Life's one bloody joke to you.'

'Oh. Touchy, touchy. And little Derek not behaving himself then?' At the look on Shirley's face, the words turned sour in Glenys's mouth.

'I haven't been out with Derek since last Thursday,' Shirley bit the words into pieces, '…if its any business of yours. And don't be so sarky!'

'Come on then Shirl, out with it. Gypsy Rose Glenys knows all, sees all…'

'You're doing it again,' Shirley cloaked her eyes, 'He stood me up again last night.'

'Again?' said Glenys, 'You never told me about the first time.'

'Well, he just passes it off in the morning at work, says 'Mornin' Shirl' and smiles like he's pinched the cats milk. I daren't say anything. I wouldn't want the other girls to think I was bothered, would I?'

Glenys watched the fruit salad disappearing one rapid chunk after another.

'I got him in the stock room this morning and said, 'What's up, don't you fancy me anymore?' He says 'Sorry Shirl, you're a nice girl and that, but you're a bit too, well, different, for my taste.' I ask you? Me! Different!'

Glenys couldn't help but smile.

'He says I'm too straight.'

Glenys nearly fell off the chair.

'No, stop it,' said Shirley, 'He didn't want his mates to see us out, and me dressed like that!'

It was the gold ring in her nose that really broke Glenys up the next lunchtime.

That evening the park was littered by a fine white frost. It haloed the moon, glinted along the rail that held the swings and stole the colour from the grass. The ducks were asleep amongst the reeds of the little island in the boating pond and a thin film of ice surrounded the boats moored there.

Glenys was warm. She'd taken Aunt Mavis' advice and let a little of the cold in. With the love she still held for her father and the memory of his laughter, she'd turned it into the good man walking beside her. She'd never hide behind her smile again. Her Doc Martens matched his Cuban heels stride for stride and never felt one inch out of place.

They met Shirley at the gate, shivering in her leather skirt and fishnets, her feet tapping circles in the frost. The studded jacket twinkled star-like in the streetlights.

'What time is it?' Glenys asked.

'Half past eight.'

Glenys reassured her, 'He'll be here soon.'

Shirley shuffled her boots in the frost.

'It really doesn't matter.'

Norman tugged gently on Glenys's arm.

'I'll be going then,' she said.

'Whatever you want,' snapped Shirley.

Norman put his arm around Glenys's shoulder and drew her closer as they walked up the park in silence. The gravel crunched resentfully beneath their feet. She slipped her arm around his waist as far as she could reach. Norman's hand made for the change in his trouser pocket.

Glenys beat him to it.

Tiger Moth

In my teens and early twenties I was an inveterate (and annoying) motorcyclist. I couldn't afford a fast one so I did what all others do in the circumstances, make it a loud one.

Alright, so the sound and the roar are just fantasies, but they aren't always. It was on an early visit to Cadwell Park that I first heard the almighty thump of a Manx Norton through an unsilenced exhaust. In the age before these bikes were relegated to 'Vintage' racing, they, the BSA Gold Star and the like, were the affordable staple bikes of the amateur racer.

I didn't know nor care who won that day, all I remember from it is the start line, where twenty bikes leapt into snarling life almost simultaneously and the air around me shook with a vibrancy I have never recaptured.

I own up to being the youth in this story, to the extent that a bloke up the road came out one day waving a table leg at me and shouting the very same words as in the story. He was a big bloke. I slowed down... but then I never was as brave as Bella...

Tiger Moth

'Next time he comes up the street like that again on that bloody motorbike, I'll bloody 'ave 'im!' I used to say.

What Bella used to say, was that it was my fault.

I'd say, 'What?' and she'd say, 'If you hadn't been so good at what you did in the war, then he wouldn't be here to upset you,' and I'd think for a moment… and say, 'No, and neither would you.'

I stopped him one day when Bella was out shopping. He gave me some right lip. Bella came home and I told her what he'd said. She said she was surprised that he'd spoken back like that to such a well-oiled killing machine.

'Listen here,' I said, 'Next time he comes blasting up the road like a maniac I'll shove that old table leg right through his spokes.'

Bella said it didn't have spokes. They all had alloy wheels now.

'Look,' she said, '…if it upsets you so much, get in the shed and… you know.'

I did know… but I didn't approve.

'Here,' she said, 'We can't all be good at everything. You had your Spitfires.'

'Tiger Moths,' I said, 'Fairey Swordfish. Never got my hands on a… Spitfire.'

'All't same,' she said, 'Aeroplanes. They shoot at people.'

'Not enough,' I said, as he blasted that bloody bike up the road again.

'Aah,' said Bella, 'But you did it so *he* could be free. So get in that shed and take the covers off. We'll sort him.'

And that we did.

I went down the cellar and took out this old wooden box. When I opened it, I'd forgotten that I'd greased and wrapped each individual spanner. I carried them upstairs and Bella smiled but kept on knitting, the needles batting like insect wings.

'Here,' I said, and pushed her hearing aid back in. She shrugged her shoulders and popped it back out again.

'You're going in the shed, aren't you?' she said, 'Do me a favour and leave it out.'

I'd lost the memory of how little light there was in the shed, and how many pigeons had been in. I held my breath and dragged off the covers. When the dust cleared, instead of the rust I'd been expecting, there was this dull gleam escaping from under a quarter inch of grease. I pulled the bike out into the garden and ran in to tell Bella. She took the battery out of her hearing aid and smiled.

It came up like a dream. I put it in gear and pulled it back against what I hoped was compression. It hesitated, and then the huge flywheel turned it over. I listened for the expected grind of steel on steel but it was as sweet as a nut. I took the plug out of the cylinder head and turned the engine over with the back wheel. The magneto was still alive. It cracked the biggest, fattest, bluest spark you ever saw.

I fetched Bella and we siphoned petrol from the car and found some engine oil on the shelf in the garage. She pushed me up and down the path until it fired. Jeesus. You never heard anything like it. Not for years anyway. Bella found the old helmet under the stairs where we'd stuffed it out of sight. Memories, you see. Not all bad ones, but we had to put away temptation while the kids were growing up. She'd hid all the trophies at the back of the china cabinet so they didn't ask questions, and the bike in the shed was… just the bike in the shed. Know what I mean?

Anyway, I ran it around the block a few times until this young git with the Kanaswaki or whatever it is comes running out of the passage shouting.

'Hey! Granddad! My dad says next time you come up the street like that again on that bloody motorbike, he'll bloody 'ave you!'

I stopped in the middle of the road and closed the throttle until it ticked over just marginally quieter than a 14 pound Howitzer. I could see the sunlight bouncing in the windows of the houses as the shockwave hit.

Mrs Wilkins from over the road shouts, 'Hey! Turn that bloody thing off!'

So I did. Not wishing to be antisocial like. No more than fixing torpedoes to the bottom of a Fairey Swordfish so they could go out and sink boats full of people. I shut off the petrol and let the motor fade, reminding myself of the bucket of green dye I was keeping by the door for the next time her Persian got out.

This git from up the road slouches and sidles his way down the hill and says, 'Alright then, Granddad. What's that?'

The bike's cooling under me, all the bits settling like cutlery thrown in a drawer.

'Don't you know, lad?' I said, 'Call yourself a motorcyclist?'

'No,' he said, 'I'm a Biker. An' if I knew what that was, I'd be a bloody archaeologist. So what is it?'

'It's a 500cc Manx Norton,' I tell him, '1947, Featherbed frame, Roadholder forks, Full Race tune, straight through megaphone exhaust.'

'What's that do?' he says.

I smiled, 'It beats you.'

'In yer dreams, Granddad,' he says.

'No, son,' I told him, 'In *your* nightmares.'

'Bet you I can do the M67 roundabout and back before you,' he says.

'You're on,' I told him, 'Sunday morning, eight o'clock.'

That Sunday me and Bella were up at the crack. By the time he turned up I was astride the bike, halfway up the hill. Bella was knitting and watching from the window.

He pulls up alongside and says, 'Go on then… kick it up.'

'Can't,' I say, 'I have to bump it.'

'I take back archaeologist,' he says, 'Palaeontologist more like.'

I swung it around and freewheeled down the hill, then dropped the clutch. The exhaust leapt into a prehistoric snarl. I coaxed and warmed it into a tick-over that I knew would rouse Mrs Wilkins in under five seconds.

'Here,' I shouted, as he pulled up alongside me, 'Hold this a minute, I need a pee.'

'Crappin' yourself, more like, Granddad,' he shouts, as I leave him holding one end of the handlebar. He waves with his other hand to Bella knitting away there in the window.

A few minutes later, face mask on, goggles fitted, helmet fastened and tight, the cracked old leathers creaked once more over the saddle. He raised his thumb, let go of the Norton and shot off.

The Norton rolled slowly at first, gathering power under it until the clutch stopped slipping then, like a thing possessed, it leaped and roared and shook the air, gathering the road under its wheels into a seamless strip of sound as it thundered ever faster towards his disappearing tail light.

The knitting lay silent as moth-wings on the window sill, needles piercing the ball at right-angles.

They were gone for hours. I didn't dare ring the police. She had no tax, test, insurance or anything except, like me, old age and long memories.

They came back in an ambulance, Bella wincing in sympathy as she helped the young git down the step, encased as he was in plaster from left toe to hip.

'I'm sorry,' said Bella, 'You shouldn't have tried to catch me on the roundabout at that speed. They're not made for it these days. I'd forgotten why we'd put ours away. Perhaps it's an age thing.'

She's been gone over a year now. But that was just like her, apologising to somebody for the trouble their own gob had got them into. I got the trophies back out since she went.

Here. That was her favourite. It's inscribed on the bottom,

'Bella 'Tiger Moth' Dunwoody'
'Fastest Woman on The Island'
'Douglas, Isle Of Man. 1949'

Fingerbowls & Filét Knives

Stories can be itemised, dissected and their ingredients brought forth as a recipe for success (or failure), so I tend not to analyse my work too often in case I discover something either nastily repetitive or so good that I can't then get my head out of the door.

But have you ever wondered about people being the ingredients of Life? The tall, lean, ascetic Asparagus amongst us? The infamous Couch Potato? The Wispy Lettuce? (We've all met *her*.) The Garlic? (Invariably too tall, with a rucksack and anorak and sat in front of me in the cinema). What kind of a recipe could you make from the people you know?

Now, Hilda is an inveterate cook. Her repertoire of dishes is as wide as her repertoire of men. They have become the ingredients of *her* life, cracked, boiled, processed, chopped or baked, in some way she has assimilated them all into her experience.

But who is on the menu tonight?

Fingerbowls & Filét Knives

The problem with Patrick, as Hilda recalled, was that it took so much of the Guinness to loosen him up, it loosened all of him up at once... and a woman has to have a handle on a man... somewhere.

With a sudden shyness of smile she recalled the night she'd joined him instead of complaining. By 10 o'clock they were barred from three pubs then rolled out of the Dubbalin Man onto the pavement in a sharp shower of vitriol and giggles, fighting with soft fists through the warm summer rain, biting slack-mouthed at one another's faces and the laughter from their wet eyes gurgling along with the water down the gutter. She hadn't had so much fun since... well... a broken leg in '74 sprang to mind.

She added half a pint of stout to the pan as her thoughts returned to Patrick. Dark and fiery-eyed, he'd been. Slender and darting as a ferret. Watched his backside as if the Devil was after him, once sober. Nerves tight as the skin on a bodhran.

He'd lurched out of Mooney's into her arms one Friday night as she was passing. She'd taken one long look in those darkly-blazing eyes and nearly dropped him. They'd held each other off the pavement for a moment and suddenly it seemed like a good idea to hang on and perhaps if they let go they might just both fall over. Later, only one of them did.

Hilda dropped the lard into the bowl where its grey bulk reminded her instantly of Frank. It wasn't the extra fat, it was the way she knew she would have to scrape it from her fingers. He'd had a way of holding on. An arm around your waist was wonderful, but when you felt it suddenly tighten at the approach of another man, any other man, it began to be a little disconcerting. And by the time they'd got to playing 'Twenty Questions' about where she'd been all day, she decided enough was enough. It took a while longer to convince Frank.

It had felt sinister being a prisoner in your own home, afraid to pick up the phone when it rang. Josie would let it ring twice then dial again. When Hilda answered, she would say *This is Fünf speaking'*.

The flour poured silently over the lard, eight silken ounces of pure George; night-club tan, ghostly and slippery, pouring like dust through her fingers. If only he could have stuck a little, had a touch of Frank about him. She recalled the night she'd found him sat in a corner of the club, hiding from the Bingo. She could have told him. There's no escape from Bingo. He'd called her a couple of times, his voice subdued on the other end of the phone and the block always on the ring-back. *'Watch him'* Josie had said, *'Teflon coated, that one.'*

How she hated it when her sister was right. She rubbed in the lard until the flour congealed into soft, rubbery, sticky lumps, kneaded in the milk then beat them angrily together with a wooden pin before rolling them roughly into shape across the dusted table.

She slid the cutlery drawer from under the table and without looking took out the filét knife with its lovingly-steeled, wickedly-concave stiletto blade that in her hand was capable of parting even that most unwilling of joints. The ribs of the cord binding impressed themselves deep into the palm of her hand from where she knew it would never slip, no matter how wet it became.

The anger left her slowly then, returning a smile to her face as she scraped the carrots then chopped them into wheels across their length, chanting all the while... *'George, Henry, Frank... George, Henry, Frank...'* as the carrots grew shorter.

For old times sake she threw a whole one into the colander, remembering Jack.

She arranged the meat into strips, trimmed like the rows of muscle that had bound Simon's stomach, closed her eyes for a moment and remembered how they'd felt, hard against her spine or pushing ridges into her softer belly. She'd counted them with slick fingers and dreamed of them long after his six-pack had turned into Boddingtons.

She'd gone with him to the gym for a while, but the aerobics felt like giving birth stood up and although she'd enjoyed the bike, she thought it should have been fitted with landscapes on a scrolling screen. Majorca would've been nice. Full of lush hills and rolling men or... rolling hills and lush men. Once the knife was in her hand, Hilda didn't care either way.

She took out the warmed earthenware dish that had reminded her so often of Michael with its glazed bronze exterior and the inside so vacuous and pale, sucked clean by an ego that wouldn't make allowances for imperfections, however minor and, more especially, hers. That was where *he'd* taken her, Majorca. Well, sort of. She'd paid the flights and he'd got the apartment. As it turned out he'd borrowed it from a friend. Complained about it the whole fortnight. Sheets too heavy. Walls the wrong colour. Plates chipped. *And* only enough full sets of cutlery for two. It wasn't as if he'd paid for it. And there *were* only two of them, yet every night he'd set a third place at the table with the mismatched and broken cutlery and adamantly refuse to say who else he'd been expecting. And no, she hadn't ever thought of having her boobs lifted. And no, she hadn't ever thought of anyone having a nose job. Not until she broke *his*, that is.

The water from the tap ran cold and clear across her hands, bouncing sparks of sunlight from the stainless bowl under the window. Outside, the sky lit clean and blue... fading at tomorrow's edge to cerise while the flower-heads burned with a slow auburn fire in late sunlight, gently nodding, just like... she stood quietly for a second, the onion gripped tightly in her left hand, filét knife in her right, eyes filling with tears. There was only *one* man could do this and... she *wouldn't* remember his name... although she could feel the thought screaming inside this locked-away place like a starving animal. No. He was there... and there he would stay.

Forever.

She stopped for a moment and listened as the screaming grew louder inside her head until her eyes over-spilled and the tears flowed a river along her cheeks and down her neck into the top of her blouse where they collected in bright, glistening pearls along the chain that held the locket that contained... well... she hadn't looked in there for a while, either.

She felt the pressure inside her lessen with the flow of the tears and shook them away with a wry smile. She looked down at the onion in her left hand and realised that she hadn't yet broken the skin. It had been *that* long since she'd thought... of Tim.

The potatoes were lumpy and very much Donald. At first hard and unyielding then later, when she applied the heat, giving and crumbling, softening away all the textures that had drawn her to him in the first place. The darkly calloused exterior, the honesty of his scarred and pitted fingernails. At first he'd just tidied himself up a bit. Then he started to blend into the shape he'd thought she wanted. Just to please her.

Men never understand, she thought, that when a woman complains you're a bit rough, it sometimes means... she's enjoying it... or... that she isn't. It's a curious thing about men, is that, thought Hilda, yet women understand it perfectly. She twisted the eyes out of a large potato with the tip of the knife. It's strange how they can't see, she thought.

She cut some of the pastry and lined the dish with it, offering Michael some substance for once. The stock with the meat and Guinness steamed night-dark across it as she spooned. Simon and Patrick would have loved that. They could have drunk and fought and regaled each other with manly-mendacious tales of heroic feats of prodigious consumption, and Patrick could have sung the tears out of them with his dark, Irish eyes and his dark, Irish songs of conflict and injustice and the lolling tongues of wronged men... usually carried in the wrong pubs in the wrong part of town at the wrong time of night. And maybe Simon would have had to fight back for some of his earlier discipline and maybe… just maybe… they might have both looked a little better in the daylight. She watched as the strips of meat swam like red mullet, swift and marinating beneath the dark foam-flecked liquid.

The potatoes shrank into the cold water where a handful of salt blanched their unseeing eyes. They would wait a while. Like the call she had promised Donald.

The carrot wheels quenched their glow like deep, smoky, setting suns where they fell beneath the surface of the gravy. She placed the whole one in a corner of the dish and marked the edge of the pastry with a thumbnail so that she would remember where it was. The onions rose like tiny, silver-crescent moons above the dark foam, sailing like a thousand ocean nights drawn and woven seamlessly into one. Maybe *this* one. The dish slid onto the third shelf of a warm oven.

She picked up three Henrys from the rack in the fridge, cracked the first into a saucer and saw immediately the way he had towered above the crowds in Istanbul. She cracked the second… remembered his 'high forehead' gleaming with sweat in the brilliant sun, as gold capped as any minaret, and him calling her name out loud like her own personal muezzin.

She'd dyed her hair a bright, platinum blonde for the holiday and found herself besieged by the Turkish men. From breakfast to nightfall she was awash with attention. They didn't care that she was giving a little in all the wrong places, or that she woke in the morning feeling lumpy and difficult in the heat. They just pushed themselves close to her so that they could gently chafe her with their own bodies, or trick their musk-dark fingers through her hair.

In the restaurants they circled her with bright, lemon-scented fingerbowls, so they could watch the refraction of her red nails against the opalescent china. In the Market she found herself whisked along by small crowds of men and boys, the boys briefly daring to touch her hands and all of them fascinated by the pale blue in her eyes.

She had so many offers that holiday, if only she'd known what they were. They disappeared like smoke when Henry turned up. The young men began laughing behind their hands and chattering along the side streets and alleys, taking away their beautiful high-pitched voices and avoiding the darkly-broken glass in the stares of their mothers and wives.

The third egg was off.

The cheese was hard and grated into the bowl the way the constantly recurring emptiness of her life grated on her nerves, shredding them noiselessly until she felt scattered and alone at the bottom of a Pyrex bowl from which there was no escape unless someone tipped you out, and from where you could see all of life passing you by forever, just out of reach, in a place where the contact and the whispers couldn't penetrate the thick glass of isolation. She longed for that strange and noisy land inside her heart that lifts then quietens with the passing of each relationship… as if it were wind raised by a good meal.

She cracked a fresh Henry into the bowl, used the rest of the pastry and lined the flan dish.

When the potatoes had boiled, she threw in the butter and hot milk then mashed them purposefully into a bland, amorphous cream. Opening the oven door, she lifted out the dish where the shades of Patrick and Simon fought and bubbled beneath a dark Guinness haze under a thousand slit moons as if the best night of their lives would last forever and daylight never beckon with its stark, bony finger.

The sharp brown glaze that had reminded her unerringly of Michael carried the bubblings and the hissing ferment as imperturbably as she had known it would. And she realised suddenly that was where the real problem had been. After she had broken his nose he had just walked away, holding himself and his ego in with both hands and the blood pouring down between his fingers and his new and permanent indifference pouring across her from the way he walked, and the way he ignored her voice.

All she had really wanted was a reaction. Perhaps a slap. Perhaps something, in fact... *anything*. Anything that would have made her feel that she was a real person, instead of an accessory. Like an old handbag. Or a pair of discarded shoes in the bottom of a wardrobe, in the back of the bottom of the wardrobe, in the deepest, darkest, dustiest recesses of an old and forgotten, unlocked and misplaced-key of a wardrobe. Where *anything* might have opened the door... but nothing ever did.

She scraped the potatoes onto the top of the meat and vegetables and smoothed them over with the back of a fork. She drew the fork across making raised lines, then again at right-angles to the first, raising them into little peaks that would brown in the silent roar of the oven in just the way she wanted them to. Peeled, boiled, mashed, shaped and browned. All with no resistance. Suddenly and inexplicably, the thought drained away all sense of achievement.

He eats well, she thought, watching him a moment before clearing away the pie dish they had almost emptied. On a sudden impulse she had left the corner with the whole carrot untouched as if reserving Jack, or at least his memory, for later. Perhaps for lunch tomorrow, where, expecting to be alone as usual, she could savour the thought for that small moment without disturbance.

She'd found Jim at the tea-dance, where he'd promised to slide her around the floor on feet of oiled silk, which he did but... not entirely. He had driven her home... finding ways across town that she herself had never dreamed existed. It was quicker that way, he'd said, but it wasn't. Not entirely. And now here he sits on my sofa, thought Hilda, full of my best pie but, and the thought entered her head unbidden, perhaps not entirely.

The cheese tart sat pale and lamenting on the hob, waiting for the heat of a supper oven. Waiting for him to say that he would stay awhile.

She watched him secretly from the kitchen as he reclined into the sofa, allowing it to envelop his tall, slender frame with its warm, leather skin. She slid out the cutlery drawer from its slot in the table and wondered if he would stay the night.

Without looking, she grasped the handle of the filét knife that had never, ever... despite so many near-misses... slipped from her hand.

Of course he would stay...

A man can always find room for a little old tart.

Firelight on Dark Water

What if you were given a gift... only to find that you were also a gift, being given. How much of your heart and self would you share? All of it? What moments in your life would you readily forget?

Would being given as a gift change the way you saw an act that you had just committed? Would it give you that second chance to reconsider from a position you thought far too late?

Gothic, erotic, poised in that limbo between here and forever, this story takes place on the one night a year when gifts are set free.

Are you the giver, the given... or the recipient? Or are we all three at one time? Take your own time. Think about it, while that special night passes, and the necessary warmth of human contact becomes a shared experience.

It's cold outside.

There's a fire in the hearth.

Change is possible without regret.

And love of self is deeper than the darkest water.

Firelight on Dark Water

He awoke as if after a long voyage, neither knowing nor caring from where he had arrived, to find himself swaying gently on the soft, salt-sea of her. He smiled where she couldn't see it, but his face kept its warmth.

She watched him as he turned to look up and saw only the smile that he'd kept while asleep then, as his face cleared, increasing, where his slowly opening eyes saw how kind the lines had been around her eyes and mouth.

He closed his eyes again to listen to the ocean of breath he could hear breaking and turning inside her. She smiled in return and he turned away, pressing his face into her breasts, floating in the warmth of the soft body beneath him.

She touched him with fingers spread, distracted by the scent of him, stroking his lean limbs and spidering her hands across his drum-tight skin.

He moaned softly and pushed himself against her hands in his hunger for contact. He pulled himself further up her body until the wild, dark crown of his hair rested against the fold of her chin. He settled against her, fitting inside the spread of her arms. Before disappearing into sleep he glanced, briefly, as his cupped hand covered her nipple. He touched it with the tip of his thumb and saw it pucker erect in the instant the darkness came to take him.

She lay there, counting neither minutes nor hours as he slept. He turned infrequently, and each time that he did she found new ways to hold and to touch him in places she had never thought would exist for her, with this man here, whose crooked arm pushed under his head gave off the scent of a river, now deep within his blood, and whose hair shone with fire-strands in the darkness.

She placed a hand each side of him and compressed him gently, her fingers searching for the vault of vast energy she had found and tapped in him. Her body felt him begin to stiffen against her. She took the hands she had placed at his sides and lifted him gently, further against her, until he rested unknowingly at the foot of her mount.

He made an involuntary movement in his sleep. Her mouth opened, closed again slowly as her breath settled to rock him gently on the crest of her, amidst the reeds and rushes of her living. She wrapped him with her arms and closed her eyes.

He stirred awake to find the room in almost darkness, the embers of the fire strung with a membrane of fabric from his ruined socks she had thrown there, the warp and weft flung between two log ends, fluctuating gold and red as the chimney drew air, scattering fire-shapes.

Beneath the window stood a bench, heavy with pots of bright colours and brushes, fresh shavings and small parts of toys littering the floor. He stretched out to touch the wall beside the bed where it seemed to absorb the light that flicked upon it, chafing dark holes in the solidly-aged timber. But as ancient as the timber was, the warmth from the fire and their bodies released from it something energetic until the room filled with the faint scent of pine.

He lifted his hand into her hair. A glow of fire shone from within it... the light writhing around his fingers.

He turned for comfort and, as his skin lifted from hers, it left a faint dampness between them that reminded him in some way of deep water.

As he moved he found that a part of him was inside her and that his movement lifted a scent from her, too, that mingled with the pine from the walls and the ash from the fire to make his head spin and his body move like an automaton.

She awoke to his eyes closed, but his wire-taut body strung above her and his skin burning within her hands. She held him as he shuddered against her, increasing her grip until they became still.

They lay quiet then, the water of his effort trickling slowly between them, filling her dimples and folds, collecting in the hollows of his back until they were studded with small lagoons that evaporated slowly in the drying warmth.

They lay watching nothing, as time stretched imperceptibly around them. He looked up to see if thoughts of maybe and when would play across her face and found only himself, reflected in the age-old mirror of her eyes.

'Tell me what you remember,' she said.

He screwed up his face, the fire-light branding lines into his youth.

'It's hard,' he said, then smiled quickly, 'Perhaps I can only remember you.'

'Try.'

The touch of her fingers relaxed his face, allowing his thoughts to float freely as willow fronds sensing a deep pool.

'I remember a bridge,' he said, 'The dark night around me and the bell that broke the eve of Christmas... my fingertips...' he looked at his hands, '...then a rush of wind. Snow on cold water... but that's all.'

'No,' she said, '...there must be more than that.'

'I changed...' he said, '...but they wouldn't...'

He held his fingertips into the firelight, examining the betraying ridges cast by deep scars and flays.

'Changed what?'

'My mind,' he said.

He turned his hands away to stare at their backs and the prominent veins pulsing there. He shook his head to escape the memory that pried at his consciousness, forcing himself to concentrate on the mantelpiece over a fire where the embers seemed locked forever in this dying, flickering light, where only this moment and his thoughts surrounding this woman seemed solid, and saw the empty, heavy wool stockings hanging there, their tops trapped under a brass candlestick.

'He's missed you this year.'

'He misses no-one,' she said.

He settled against her, his movement slick against the still-dampness of her skin. She prodded him with her voice.

'There's more than that.'

He shrugged his whole body wilfully.

'I can't remember.'

She ran one finger along the length of his spine and chuckled softly as he shuddered against her.

'You can. You just don't want to.'

He shuddered again.

'It was a girl,' she said, teasing pain into his thoughts.

He shook his head, trying to locate some shred of clear reason behind the way this room and this ancient yet still beautiful woman filled his mind with strange and comfortable warmths and knowing scents, and the way the fire drilled his muscles and moved him against her but, knowing also… as his brain shifted slowly in the mist… that he would wish to keep this time forever.

He nodded.

She stroked the moist hair that darkened his head and framed his eyes.

'It was a girl,' she said, 'It's always a girl. A *foolish* girl.'

At that he looked up, a question illuminating his face.

'A man always seems to find a girl,' she said, '…at the moment he most needs a woman.'

He turned his face away and in the absence of an answer his body seemed to shrink in upon itself while his hands admired her, taking every place upon her into themselves, planting beneath their skin the shapes and sharp tangs of her electricity, her beautiful roundness of being, and the softly folded comfort of her.

She looked to the window where the slight crack of curtain showed a sky as faded as the knees of his jeans, now dry and crisping by the fire, and saw the high stars washed away in a tip of light no stronger than the scent of pine in the room and the water flowing between their bodies.

'It's time,' she said.

He stretched alongside her and moaned gently in the back of his throat. She felt his breath quicken once and stark inside of him and knew he was becoming fully awake.

He rolled away from her and rose to sit on the edge of the bed. He placed his head in his hands and massaged his temples.

She took the sheet from the bed and with great gentleness wiped his body dry in the last of the light from the embers before wrapping it around herself.

'Take the socks,' she said.

He looked to the window and saw, as she had, the faint crack of daylight riding the stars, although the darkness still inhabited the trees clinging fiercely to the ground.

'There's still time.'

'It's alright,' she said, 'Take the socks. They're yours.'

He reached them down from the mantle.

'They're empty.'

She looked at him in the gathering gloom, saw the concern behind his eyes and smiled.

'He misses no-one.'

'But on this morning,' he said, 'on *this* of *all* mornings, they should be full.'

'Then... put them on,' she said.

He stepped into the socks and found they fitted. He knocked the smell and stiffness of black water from the jeans and shirt where they had been drying by the fire and put them on.

He came back to sit beside her on the bed. He felt her body flow against him inside the white river of the sheet. He touched her hair, her face, reached out but she caught his fingers in hers and led them gently away until they lay entwined between them on the bed.

'Shall I ...love you?' he began.

'No,' she replied, 'Learn to love yourself instead, and you won't ever need to come back.'

She watched the bright expectation of half-hope fall within his face.

'This is my Gift,' she said, 'Given twice it serves only to halve the first joy.'

He nodded in return, not wanting to accept, but feeling the air of finality with which she suddenly filled the room. He bent to kiss her lips for the last time. She returned him in full measure and they parted slowly.

'He will be here soon,' she said.

He stood quickly and crammed his feet with the new socks into the boots he'd found beneath the bed. The leather was hard and stiff and he flexed them as he stood. He took down the coat from the back of the door and brushed the river-bed dust from it with the back of his hand.

She pulled her knees up against her and for a moment buried her face in the sheet wrapped around them.

He turned slowly. She looked up and waved him away.

'He'll be waiting.'

He looked around the room and attempted to fill his sudden, clamouring emptiness with the immortality of the log walls and their hidden, secret darkness... the mantelpiece now shorn of socks... the tall dry candlestick... and discovered a new scent of himself amongst the sheets and the fragrance of cold river and pine, and if that was all he was leaving behind, he found himself taking away so much more.

She watched as his hand gave the doorknob a half turn, as his feet hesitated on the mat, as his face turned towards hers, until she met him there with a smile.

'It's alright to change your mind,' she said, taking his hand one last time in hers. He studied her skin, and for a moment saw the stretch, tighten and glaze where a hard fire had brushed against it.

She withdrew her hand, 'He makes it right. You'll see.'

He looked down at his own guilty fingertips to find them healed, strong, fresh and capable.

The door closed softly behind him. The trees outside became dark, cloying things, resisting the early light with their subtle twists of branches, black in the cold air. The snow beneath his boots searched for the heat of his body, but the socks held him safe and warm.

He tightened the coat around him and walked away without once looking back.

A stooped figure in a red hunting suit waited a short distance from the house. As the youth approached, the man removed a mitten and held out his hand. Their fingers embraced; the youth's strong but slender, the man's hard and rough, skin stiffened from exposure to eternal cold. He held open a low door into the sleigh and the youth stepped in to sit on the small wooden seat. The man eased in beside him and took up the reins.

With the barest whisper of harness and hoof the reindeer lifted into the sky, turning their heads towards the new morning, away from where... flowing along the horizon... ran the deep, dark, changeless water of night.

M'Aidez, M'Aidez

This story was born out of a workshop with my great friend, Berlie Doherty. As well as being an incredibly accomplished writer of Children's and General Fiction, Berlie is an excellent motivator and workshop leader.

The workshop was held in Berlie's beautiful English country cottage in Derbyshire, and our remit was to go for a walk around the local area and return for lunch and formulate a story from our experiences.

As I walked around with Bryony, my partner, I could hear the others chattering away from some distance, their voices ebbing and flowing. All the elements in the story are things that we found while exploring, (except the delightful Emma), and they are all here on the page.

'M 'aidez', 'M 'aidez'

'It's a Mayfly.'

'No, it isn't.'

'Yes it is.'

Emma was bone tired of listening to the chatter rolling like loose stones in their mouths.

'You wouldn't know a Mayfly if it jumped up and bit you,' she said.

'Yes, I would,' replied Dave.

'Alright,' said Bob. He stepped out onto a black, moss covered rock that parted the stream, sending some of it shingling into the shallow bank where Emma sat.

'How would you know it's a Mayfly?'

'Well, I don't know anything else that lives under rocks,' said Dave.

Bob jumped back onto the shingle and together, he and Dave edged their way upstream along the pebbled margin.

Their voices fell around the loop of the river, echoed and sepulchral, to where Emma sat, tasting the scent of newly disturbed grass while the chill of swiftly churning shallow water wrinkled the skin of her toes. She remained silent and still, listening to them silvering the black stones with their lack of wit and the incessant liquidity of their babbling.

'Does that make it a Mayfly, then. Just because it lives under a rock?'

Emma lifted her toes from the water, feeling the sunlight warm and golden on the softened skin, then dipped them back in, spreading them wide so that a new sound hissed from the quiet shingle beneath the surface. The voices came once more.

'Look. There's a tin.'
'It's not. It's a can.'
'It's a tin!'
'It's a can!'
'Alright, what's it say on it?'
'Can't quite make it out, but I think it's a lager.'
'That does it then. If it's beer it's a tin.'
'Unless it's canned beer.'

Emma leaned back and felt the shingle bite through the thin cotton of her T shirt into the early summer pale glow of her skin and for a moment it was quiet, like the country should be. Then the voices found her again, buzzing her ears as if they were sheep flies.

'There's a fish in it!'
'In what?'
'In the can.'
'You mean …in the tin.'
'Tin. Can. Whatever.'

'Well, it's natural, innit?'

'What is?'

'Well, it's another example of Man hand in hand with Nature, innit? I mean, if somebody hadn't thrown in the can …tin …the fish wouldn't have had nowhere to live, would it?'

'Yeah. Stands to reason that, dunnit?'

'Yeah. This conservation's all bollocks, innit?'

Emma heard their hard-soled city shoes tramp the little plank bridge like two thirds of Billy Goats Gruff, all the while hoping for a Troll. Their voices tapered off through the ferns as they climbed the short rise to the field above.

Two foxgloves stood out on the crest, pale, pink and rude. The only difference, she thought, was the silence. The IQ was about the same.

She knew exactly where they were as the voices found her again, coming through the break in the grey limestone wall that ridged the far bank. She stood up and stretched in the warm light, watching the motes and pollen drifting close by the water where the sun shafted through the higher branches. It wouldn't be long now. She racked the sun against the tops of the trees and measured the length of the shadow of her arm with a quick glance. Half an hour until the bus. Maybe a bit more.

'It's still alive, innit.'

'Can't be.'

The river of inanity began to swell again as they reached the uprooted tree. Emma heard it flood and ripple with nonsense and ridicule, the arguments as fatuously clear as the stream beneath the bridge.

'It is.'
'But it's ripped out of the ground.'
'Perhaps it's a Lightning Tree.'
Emma searched the sky for clouds and wished.
'But trees are supposed to be stood up.'
'Give us a hand then.'
'Don't be a pillock all yer life, it's too big.'

Emma began to climb the bank at the far side of the bridge. Every time her foot slipped she remembered a reason why this had seemed like a good idea at the time. Well, Dave was good looking, but he'd insisted on bringing Bob along with them. Still, she'd thought, if I can get them out into the country, perhaps …except now she wasn't sure quite what she'd thought, and this certainly wasn't anything like she'd expected.

By the time she topped the rise they'd found the old van. Dave was stood in the wreck, swinging the steering wheel and waving. Bob picked his way amongst the skeletal steel remains, his movements small, quick and vulture-like. Dave thumped the horn button, as if that would make up for the lack of electricity. He hooted his discovery.

'It's a Ford.'
'It in't.'
'It is.'
'It in't.'

Emma climbed lazily onto the horizontal branches of the fallen tree. She hitched her way along the trunk until she reached the huge vertical disc of roots entwined with rock where it had ripped from the earth. She turned, leaned her back against it, and watched them despairingly while she considered the day. So far this had been a waste of her best tee shirt and her skimpiest pair of shorts. She'd hoped at least to start a bit of competition between them, but this wasn't quite what she'd had in mind.

'It is. It's a Ford Thames.'
'Are tha sure it's not a Mayfly?'
'No. That were a Triumph. Me uncle had one.'
'That were a Mayflower.'
'It weren't. It were a Mayfly.'
'Flowers don't live under rocks in a river.'
'No, you pillock, the car.'
'I've just telled thee. It were a Ford Thames.'
'Aye, I knew it were summat to do with a river.'

Emma stretched languidly along a wide, bare branch, allowing her legs to fall enticingly either side.

'Hey, look,' said Dave, ignoring them completely, 'There's names carved on this tree.'

They began to read them, wandering around beneath and totally oblivious to the soft-skinned distractions of Emma's legs, all the while laughing and chuckling at the love-hearts and promises of undying devotion. Emma decided it was only fair to ignore them too. She slid from the branch and made her way around to the other side of the tree where it fell in shade and was carved with the legends, 'Emma and Jim, May 93' and 'Emma and Scott, May 94'. Her fingers found the old scar on its low side and traced out 'Emma and Mike, May 89' and knew in that instant that it would never be carved with 'Emma and Dave' or 'Emma and Bob, May 96'.

She led the way down the bank, back over the bridge and

on to the lane where the bus would turn around and wait for a minute or two before taking her back to town, where she could at least close her own door and find a moment of silence and peace.

'That river's got iron in it,' said Dave.
'Where's it going to get iron from out here?' asked Bob.
'It's in the soil.'
'You mean, like where that old farm van's rusting away?'
'No. That orange stuff coming out of the bank.'
'Strange,' said Bob,' You'd think they'd dig it up, wouldn't you? Make something useful out of it. Like beer cans.'
'Tins.'
'And then there'd be more places for the fish to live.'
'But only if we threw 'em in.'
'Well, that's what the country's for, innit? Comin' out and drinking beer.'
'Like you said, this conversations all bollocks.'
'You mean conservation,' said Bob.
'Don't correct him when he's right,' said Emma.

The bus pulled into the end of the lane and groaned its way towards them in a low gear until it drew abreast of the turning point. As it reversed, a small stone spit out from the side of a tyre and hit Dave on the arm.
'Owww,' he said,' Something just jumped up and bit me.'
'What was it?' asked Rob.
'Don't know,' said Dave.
'That settles it then,' said Emma.

N.R.O.V.

Not Required On Voyage.

N.R.O.V. were the letters chalked onto luggage, other than cabin trunks, in the days of ocean-going liners, denoting that these could be stowed away in the hold until the ship reached its destination. A lot of these trunks held the keepsakes of a former life, perhaps out in the colonies and now returning home. Some of them must have been filled with the things deemed necessary to embark on a new stage of life. Perhaps in a land from which there would be no return journey…

What would you take, and what would you most like to throw overboard. The cat… or Mrs Wilkins?

This story is full of hang-ups. Flame-haired women, utility companies, cats, life-changes, tax, clutter and bits of paper all get equal billing here. Throw them in together and you have a man embarking on one of life's most stressful journeys.

N.R.O.V.

Look here, at the edges of these shelves where the corners have rubbed off. I was going to re-stain them but it's too late now. And this fire never got made until tea-time. Except Saturdays, then it never went out 'til Monday morning, but I've let it go out now. It's sat there full of grey ash. Still warm underneath.

Here, I'll poke it a bit. See? Still a bit of red under there. I think I'll sit and watch it. I've never seen it go out. There must be a last spark in there somewhere. I could sit and watch it swell and die, and then when I think it's gone the cat'll come in and the draught from the door'll fan it and for a second or two it'll burn bright as a star. Then nothing. Just the warmth in the grate and the sigh of the ash falling through the bars.

Matches on the mantle. Propped open by a mermaid from Cleethorpes with her hand up the bottom of the box and all the little heads poking out like a troupe of red-haired women.

Red-haired women, eh? I never went looking for trouble.

Still. Red-haired women…

Look here. Fag burns in the armchair. On the rug. On your trousers. Eee, you're a sloppy bugger. That'll all have to change. Can't afford that now. Here, look, two gas bills. Paid. One of them's for electricity. I wonder where they convert it. Must be that new pipe they laid through the front garden.

It buggered the roses all through last year but they've come good now. Bit late. But it's the way the house faces. Sun goes too high in summer. It's only now it stays low enough to miss the roof. I'd better check that I'm all packed. I won't be a minute...

Gas bills ...yes, we know about them. Council Tax ...up to yesterday. Paid. I can't read this one. Serves me right for waiting so long before I get the new glasses. Don't see why I should pay all that money when tomorrow... but that's another day.

Readers Digest. I'll see if there's enough spark left in the fire. These all used to be tucked behind the clock. But I packed that already. It's in a big box in the spare room. I wrote on it with a marker. It says N.R.O.V. Not Required on Voyage. It's tucked in with my snap bag and flask.

I closed the curtains early tonight to keep the cat out. No, no, he can get in if he wants, but he only comes in when he sees them open. Simple. Curtains open. Food. Curtains shut. Empty dish. Talking of curtains. How long have they been up? Mary took 'em and washed 'em last time. How long ago were that? March, I think, or it might have been April. I'm not sure. I know it was '96. I slipped up there. I thought I'd got everything ready. Still, what's a pair of curtains. Well, I'll tell you, it's the difference between breakfast and starvation to the cat. I wonder how long he'll last when I don't wake up one morning?

Did you know that roses don't close up at night? No? Here, look. I'll draw the curtains. Can't open the window. I've put this cling-film over them. You just stick it over then warm it up with Mrs Wilkins hair dryer. You can't tell it's on. Until you want to open the window.

Oh, look here.

Get down. I said, get down. Get off the sill! You stupid cat. You can't come in this way I've got cling film on the windows. Can't you see? Go on. Bugger off!

Oh bugger. That's torn it. Hang on, I might as well open it now.

Come on then. Come on. Here puss. Here puss. No? Oh, bugger off then...

Like I was saying, about the roses. You can't see them now because it's dark but they're all open, just like it was morning. I'll put the outside light on and you can see them.

There. See? All open. What's that bloody cat doing?

Get away from the roses. They're all marked up ready. Can't you see. Don't go digging round them now.

Oh bugger. The cling film.

Now look what you've done, cat.

It's alright, Mrs Wilkins.

That's Mrs Wilkins over there, in the bedroom window with the light on.

It's alright Mrs Wilkins, I haven't got a burglar. It's just this silly cat again.

Stop waving, Mrs Wilkins. I said you can stop waving now, I'm alright.

And for god's sake go and put some clothes on, woman.

When her arm moves there's this Mexican wave goes all the way down her body. *Uuurghh.* I'll have to draw the curtains again. She'll stand there wanting something until I do. She's worse than the cat. And look at that cat.

Get down off the wall.... Now!

I've labelled all the bulbs in those pots. *And get your tail down, you've only been done a month.*

It's alright Mrs Wilkins. It's only the cat. He's a bit like you... *still thinks he's got something to offer.*

Here puss. Here puss. That's it. Come on. Back up here, away from the bulbs and the roses. Up here on the sill where you can't pee on the geraniums. That's it. Here, tap, tap, tap. Tap, tap tap. Here, puss, puss, puss. Are you hungry? Are the curtains open? Is it making your little tummy rumble? Ahhhh. Are you saying meow out there? Do you want to come in now? Well you're not ...*so sod off.*

Oh, bugger... This cling film sticks to your hands.

Fire'll never go out at this rate.

I've got a few books here, on the shelf. I haven't packed these. It takes a while to get to know a book. If you have too many you never get to know them all, not like you should. It's like having too many children. Do you know why books have covers? It's like keeping in a secret. You see an open book lying around and you can't resist taking a peek. Just to see where it's got to, as if the pages have travelled there all on their own. But when it's shut it keeps the noise in. The noise that books make in your head. The roar of the sea and the clanging of bells and the cannons and sharp crack of wit and rifles, and cynicism that sticks in you like a barbed spear.

Some of them are full of poison and make changes inside you that you didn't want, and certainly didn't ask for when you paid your four pounds fifty or whatever. So I don't keep many around. Just in case I feel like leaving one open.

There should be a ritual for opening a book. A state of mental and physical preparation that's known only in a Buddhist monastery or somewhere, where nobody else can read. I'd better learn it. I'll need it where I'm going.

I'm going to roll this rug up. Did you know that under this rug there's a piece of carpet that hasn't seen the light of day for ten years? It looks new. The carpet had a pattern once. I'd forgotten that. But then if you look I suppose it's still hiding under the sideboard. I should have noticed it when I retrieved that piece of cheese last week. Perhaps it was under the cat hairs. I'll put a label on this. Rug... one... N.R.O.V.

Where's my list? Dentist. Cancel all existing appointments. Done.

Perhaps if I turn out the light I'll be able to see that last spark. No. I don't want to leave here in the dark. I want to go while I can see all the little bits and bobs of life up until now, well, *chucked* around me, I suppose you'd have to say. Like the cabinet behind me that's full of old letters and postcards. I went through them all last week. Hundreds of them. Never knew I was so popular... with Readers Digest. I locked it up and labelled the key N.R.O.V. and put it in the box with the clock.

Move On, they said to me last Friday.

Move On. We're all Moving On, they said, and like a river or a stream, they said, we all have tributaries and backwaters where the waters flow a little more gentle and the bones can ease out and life will extend for you like the best fishing rod you can buy. I wouldn't mind if fishing wasn't like watching paint dry.

Move On, they said. It's true, everything moves on, and they moved on and left me sat here. Last Friday seems such a long way away now, like down the wrong end of a telescope. Mind you, I've been busy since then. *Moving on.* I haven't even had time to look at the watch they gave me. It's upstairs in the box with the clock and flask. They had it engraved on the back but what with waiting until I could get free glasses I couldn't read it. Probably says, N.R.O.V.

Just a minute. The cat's at the window.

Stop scratching, will you? Can't you see the curtains are

closed? Hello, Mrs Wilkins. What? Yes. I can see I left the light on. No. Don't wave. Please... *Uuurghh*.

Did I show you the roses? Oh, yes. Let's see. What else have I got here. P45. Tax paid to date... Jeeesus. National Insurance... Jeeesus. Still, that's one club I shan't be joining again.

I'd better start getting the stuff out that I'm taking, or I won't be ready.

Shoes. Brown brogues. Six Pairs. Identical. Well you never know, and I won't get them again at this price. Look, *I* don't know how far I'm going and these are well, me, and... they're comfortable. Fashion? N.R.O.V. from now on.

Trousers. Four pairs. Dark grey twill. Got some more upstairs, they're only a slight flare. Six shirts, soft collars. None of this heavy ironing stuff.

Underpants? Eight new packs from M & S. Socks, 22 pairs pale grey. Money? Well, I won't need as much.

Oh, bugger. The fire's gone out and I missed it. And the cling film's stuck all the ash together.

Four new books. Tightly sealed in plastic bags. Until I find the right ritual. I've got this other one here, open. It's called 'Onwards and Upwards' or 'How to remain Mobile under Changing Circumstances'. It's all about.... well, I hesitate to use the word, and anyway the book tells me not to.

Look, here, where it's open. Bet you can't resist it. Have a peek, go on. It says, 'treat everything as a step forward, a continuation of life's journey into new and exciting areas of experience'. A 'New Frontier to a Strange New World'. What do they think this is? Bloody Star Trek? Anyway, I think it's time I put all my cards on the table.

Here, look... Library Card... Gold Leisure Card... Bus Pass, not valid until tomorrow, and last but not least ...Pension Book.

Listen… upstairs. Can you hear it? Bloody clock. I forgot to turn off the chimes. There it goes, …9 …10 …11 …12.

That's it then. Goodbye… Working Life.

What's that bloody cat doing rattling at the door? Can't it see the curtains are still closed? *Bugger off…*

Oh, Hello Mrs Wilkins. Yes, you're right, it is my birthday tomorrow. You've brought me a present? Not necessary, Mrs Wilkins. Well then, what is it? Oh. Mrs Wilkins! Fasten that coat back up!

Oh! Red Hair!

No! Please!

Stand still!.

Uurghhh.

And you've let the cat in.

Vayu Manush
(The Wind Man)

I wanted to write a story about rain. Not the dreary half-assed drizzle we wake up to on February mornings here in the north of England, but proper rain... the kind that means something... that makes a difference to life... the kind that washes and cleanses the land and opens our eyes to the bright and the new... the kind that breaks open the earth and begins the cycle of life over and again.

I then thought how useful it would be if there were an event that presaged that kind of rain... a thing expected, that could be planned for and experienced with a delight for the future.

The Wind Man came to me in a dream...

Vayu-Manush

Gupta awoke to a thunderclap that shuddered him from a dream in which the eggs of his chickens fell dry and empty-cracked into the bowl.

For a moment he thought that he had awoken running, chasing chickens along the twisting, empty river bed. He could even feel the dust slapping dry at the soles of his feet then, through half-slit eyes, he saw that his wife was beating his naked toes with the stick she used to separate the dogs.

'He is here!' she said.

Gupta leapt, wide-eyed, from the chair, 'He is *coming?*'

'*Aleh!*' said his wife, 'He is *here!*'

Gupta moved stiff-legged to the verandah where his delicate brown fingers steadied him against the top rail. At the far edge of the nightfall depth of forest, over which the prodigal heat of the sun rose each morning to search the tops of banyan, jackfruit and the dark secluded mangrove, a plume of dust shook the twilight stars. Flocks of bright birds moved on before it through the trees, chafing their feathers in the crack of evening, scattering the dark leaves with the chaff of their cries. A second clap of thunder vented the sky above him and the perspiration on his back turned chill as the rapidly forming clouds sucked any remaining moisture from the air.

Below him, the shout pushed on through the village.

'*Aleh!*'

...hands grasping at shallow-dented copper, fingers beating joy into rhythms with worn, wooden spoons...

'*Aleh! ...Aleh! ...He is coming!*'

Around the stilted huts, bare feet scampered the dust into a golden silt studded through with grains of discarded rice, withered banana leaves and the debris of a long, hot summer without rain.

'*Vayu-Manush,*' they cried, '*The Wind-Man... He is coming!*'

Along the single village street, hands lifted wind-chimes into favoured positions on balconies, porches and roof edges.

Fingers of all shapes and sizes strung high the brightly painted metals, dully glowing crystal and slender filaments of glass shaped and holed over years with the infinite patience of water wearing away at stone. Transomed and buttressed and sprung with bits of discarded steel rod, on slender fishing line that disappeared into the gloom in which these things hung suspended, they caught the chime and distance of the stars, until a sharp exhalation scattered them back into broken shards of glass and cold, hard, metal.

'*Aleh! ... Aleh!*'

Bhopal's wife dragged the small settee out onto the porch. It groaned with the death throes of a sundered concertina as her husband settled his huge frame into it. She carried an elaborately filigreed, brass-topped table from inside the house and set it down where his hand could reach it without expending unnecessary energy. Energy that she knew he would say could be saved for another thing, for the crops that were not dug because the ground was too hard and dry, for the bringing up of children who could better fend for themselves in the streets, and for the training of dogs that had long since learned to skitter beyond the reach of his stone.

Bhopal watched Gupta hanging his wind-chime from the edge of the porch roof.

He raised his glass of tepid tonic water, 'That is a *fine* wind-chime, Gupta,' he said.

'Thank you very much,' returned Gupta. He screwed the new metal hook into the split-bamboo gutter and hung the next cord from it.

Suspended beneath a spiderwork of bent iron crosses, six pearlescent white eggs danced and spun on thin, web-like strands. From the centre of the crosses he hung a finely-balanced flat-steel rooster, with edges filed and smooth.

Gupta had punched a hole for its eye with his finest chisel and that eye now gleamed back at him with the blue of the night air and the quick flash of an early star. He touched it with a finger. The bright red of its comb rocked and spun. The brown of its painted feathers dipped and fluttered in the light. The bright yellow of its beak pecked and pecked at the eggs as it passed, saturating the porch with the bright tinkling sound of children's laughter, far away in his memory.

'That is *indeed* a fine wind-chime,' said Bhopal, raising a glass filled with the clearest of liquids, while issuing his philosophy of the acceptance of life and its multitudinous vagaries into the still resounding air between them, 'I wish that I had one, too.'

His wife brought him a fresh glass filled with tonic from the cooling-pit she had dug beneath the house. Her clothes carried a dust, blown under the legs on which the house stood, that had followed her up through the trapdoor and into the smoke where the cheap oil lamp sputtered fitfully across the kitchen with the tongue of a wicked cat.

She placed the glass beside the others and sat away from Bhopal on a small stool by the door. From there, she watched Gupta adjusting his wind-chime. She watched his slender brown fingers twitch wires, balance bright cross-members, untangle cords invisible across the street and saw, even from that small distance, how sure his hands were, and how they moved with deference to the materiel in which they found themselves working, tuning and turning, in the growing dark.

'I wish that I had one, too,' she said.

'I say, Khalil,' shouted Gupta, 'That looks a *particularly* fine wind-chime.'

'It is new,' replied Khalil, his voice clear and distinct across the street against the hush that had grown in depth like the premonition of a bell.

'I find him something to do when it rains,' called his wife.

She held her husband's legs as he stood uncertainly upon a small table, separating strings and polished copper tubing.

'Then it must have been finished a *long* time,' said Gupta.

Brass discs shifted horizontally between Khalil's fingers, chanting dully with the movement of his hands. The chime came sonorous and deep, fruitful and melodic, echoing autumnal across the street where it teased Gupta with the smell of harvest and the dull thud of ripe fruits falling through trees to the ground. He breathed it in and the sound twitched his nose with the scent of fermenting mango and bitter-sweet pears. Nodding his silent approval, he smiled into a thought of the coming season.

'I thought I might have heard you testing it, Khalil?' he said.

Khalil cursed quietly into the gloom of hanging rafters and dark musty purlins under the porch roof where the insects worked their hidden, rhythmic lives.

His wife replied for him, her voice replete with a humour as dry as the season, 'When he had it finished he wrapped himself in blankets, so that the sound would not escape.'

She laughed easily at the memory. Gupta took up the thought and for a moment the street rang with a shared, crystal picture of Khalil, swaddled like a sick child and chiming with the dull sound of a demented clock.

'We thought it was the ghost of his father, come back to haunt us,' she said, the full richness of her voice overflowing with ridiculous images of which Gupta could see clearly every one.

'It would make a change from the Ghost of Poverty,' he replied.

'No, it wouldn't,' replied Khalil's wife, 'I think his father found a way to take his money with him. All he left behind was this fool...'

She shook Khalil's legs until the chimes rattled and sang in his grasp, '...and it seems to be worthless.'

Khalil climbed down from the table, 'Is that not the best wind-chime on the street, woman? In the village? *In the whole of Bengladar?*'

He shouted across to Gupta, 'Do not listen to this foolish woman. The only thing my father left behind was me, on my own, to live with this creature who ridicules me to the street and my friends. At least when he was alive I could have a conversation with someone who made sense.'

His wife sat down beside him on the edge of the porch, her feet tracing the dust of the street.

'Your father had no more brains than he had teeth,' she said, 'And the only thing he could chew was soup.'

Khalil looked up to where the wind-chime hung with its straight truths of copper and deceptively bright circles of brass.

'Tell me, Gupta. Is that not the finest of wind-chimes?'

'Play it for me,' said Gupta.

Khalil's fingers reached up and gently trembled the edge of a tube. From that point, the motion began. A sway took the first length, twisting it into the path of a bright brass circle that connected with another, and then another, until the rich, fruitful sound of its hidden music fell out into the street. The notes dropped like round, fat-bellied insects from the spaces in the roof to Khalil's ears where they became secret, succulent fruits wrapped in richly veined leaves, filling him with a fomentation of intoxicating pride.

'Is that not …the *finest*?' he asked, as much to himself.

'It is …the *finest,*' said Gupta, seeing now the chipped red paint of the cock-comb and the cracks appearing in the opalescent coating of the steel eggs at which his own rooster pecked, as Khalil's chimes ebbed into the dust.

A clap of thunder, almost directly overhead, split the evening sky and, in the silence that followed, the plume broke the edge of the forest, scattering animals shrieking their terror into the waiting patience of the wind-chimes.

Gupta and his wife took their seats against the house wall, far back within the shadow of the porch.

Bhopal's wife brought him a last glass from the cool shade beneath the house and sat down, the table now filled with part-empty glasses.

Khalil sat close against his wife, no longer caring who saw them in this auspicious time, this time in which she left him no secrets, as his father had said she would. Yet in the sound of the chimes it had come to him that, although she said things that seemed to shame him, he could find a token of pride hidden deep in her voice, and in the way she held him when all was still and the only noises were the animals shuffling in their loose pens and the faint, soft sounds of other people being held in houses close by. He leaned back against the house and waited.

The plume of rising air moved up the street, following its yearly-worn path along the centre where the dust gathered, rusting its colour while waiting for the cleansing power of the rain.

The wind began to gather around them, whipping gently at the clothes of Gupta and his wife and teasing Khalil, who waited, watching his chime intently for the first sign of movement.

Bhopal arranged the last, carefully-measured glass upon the table.

Entering the space between the first of the houses, the plume gathered the loose air around itself, drawing it inwards from back yards and pig pens, empty side spaces and septic trenches, plucking the feathers from shrieking chickens and sending them blending into the twisting, spinning tower.

On Gupta's porch, the chimes began to move. The rooster pecked, tentatively at first, then with a growing insistence, chipping away at the paint in a desperate attempt to free the metal chicks dangling forever almost out of his reach. Gupta's wife gripped his sleeve tightly as the rooster spun and flashed brown and red in the light, spilling, sucked out from the kitchen, into the spinning, searching winds surrounding them. He found that she was shaking, and comfortably identified the small tremors.

Bhopal's wife moved the table bearing the glasses further out onto the porch as the blistering wind whipped the dust from beneath her feet. She returned to her place beside the door, clutching to the seat of the stool as if afraid that the wind would lift her soul from her and they would be parted forever, in the way that she knew in her heart they already were.

As the wind lashed the slender wicker of the chair beneath her, it tugged at the ledges and braces of the brass-topped table, and the glasses on it began to chime. They rattled, fretting at the empty bottle in their midst, the levels of their remaining pale liquids carefully orchestrated in tonic scales and cadences, the whole rocked at once by a melodic wind.

Deeply philosophical, Bhopal issued an energetic smile.

Khalil found himself gripped hard by his wife's hand. The pain brought him back from his reverie of deep, sonorous poundings where falling cliffs of mango broke open upon the harsh stones of the land, the long tubes suspended above him brokering the distance of days between dry and empty trees and the coming season.

'Look!' she said. 'I see him.'

Khalil looked where she pointed, 'I see nothing,' he said.

'As I have said… *many times,*' she replied.

From the safety of the porch she watched as the Wind-Man pounded the street with his footsteps, each fall twisting the dry earth and wrenching it skywards, chuting it along the dark vortex of his tapering black trousers, spinning and whirling it with his dark suited arms, whisking and combining shrieks and feathers and debris up into the dark tower above him. His white hair flowed, updrafted into a mane of chimes echoing frantically from their hiding places on wind-wracked porches and roofs. The wind tore at her back where she pressed against the thin bamboo wall, urging her forwards, begging her to join in the freedom of the movement of air.

As he passed, the Wind-Man seemed to turn his face to her and she jolted with the sharp shock of recognition. Slowly, the air ceased to move, and the chimes fell gently into another year-long silence.

Full and fat bodied, the first drop of water fell into Khalil's half-sculpted bamboo gutter. He felt it roll downwards until it met the pipe. It ran from there, slickly oiled by dust, into the waiting tub. As if that single chime of rain were the signal, the war of attrition began. Bucket and bowl, tureens, balthi dishes, all clattered noisily out onto porches. Halved oil drums ricocheted beneath pipes open-mouthed and still retching summer dryness at the edges of roofs... and then it came. Crystal and cool. Tippling. Then cascading into growing percussions. Filling the air rapidly with notes of liquid lucidity, the night drowned in the plumbing of a vast orchestra, the overture of the chimes instantly forgotten in the movement of time and season marching close behind the Wind-Man.

Gupta saw how easily the rainwater slipped through his bamboo roof. He watched it run in pearls down cords, along cross-members, in bright fluid motion along fishing line into holes punched in bright metal eggs, obscuring the chipped paints and the file marks on still jagged edges, making them over and new again for the next year. He carefully lifted a brimming wooden bowl and bent his head to gently kiss the surface of the water. Lips barely wetted, he passed it to his wife who, feigning reluctance with a smile, did the same. She put it down beside her and rose gracefully. Taking his slender fingers in hers, she led him inside the hut where they would lay quietly for a while, until the shatter of rain on bamboo matched the pounding in her veins.

Bhopal reached out with a glass into the stream of water pouring through the sieve of his porch awning. He rinsed it in the flowing crystal then drank, lifting a toast to Gupta.

Khalil found himself still gripped by the shaking hand of his wife.

'I saw him,' she said.

'Saw who?' asked Khalil, shuffling bowls beneath the leaking gutters with his feet.

'*Vayu-Manush*,' she replied.

'You are a child,' he said.

'And so are you,' she replied, '...for it was your father.'

Khalil turned to look into her eyes, 'The Wind Man is *everyone's* father,' he said.

He released the grip of her fingers and folded her hands gently into his lap. From the ground arose a smell of earth sweetened by the fresh promise of the rain. He heard the soft grunt of the sow, washed clean of dust and seen anew from eyes awash with their own storm, heard the gentle thud as her forelegs gave way and her chin hit the mud, heard the muted crow of the rooster from beneath the connubial shelter of the hut, knew in his heart that tonight, as they lay together beneath the suffocating blanket of the pounding rain, he himself would shout, '*Aleh!...*', and hear its chime echo down the generations.

To Kill A Wish

...is a story about erections, loss, fading love, dead dogs, squeaking gates, envy, and Japanese Brake Parts.

Before that puts you off, I'd mention that this is the story that got me into the winners anthology of the Fish Prize, an honour I don't think I've ever bettered. And thereby hangs a tale...

I was asked to read this story at the Cork Literary Festival, only to be told by Clem Cairns, the Organiser... after I'd booked flights, accommodation etc. in the centre of Cork... that it was the *West* Cork Literary Festival, some sixty-odd miles away in Bantry. My requests for accommodation at the only room left in town was along the lines of:

'You would'na really want to stay here.'

'Yes I would.'

'There's a pub next door and they get awful drunk of a Friday.'

'Good, I intend to be one of them.'

'Don't bring a car. They sit on them outside if it's not raining.'

'I shall sit on it myself and beat them off with a stick.'

'Oh... alright then. It'll be twenty punt. Will there be just the one of you?'

'No, two.'

'Oh well...'

We got there in the end... but I never knew it could be so hard to spend money...

To Kill a Wish

I remember one morning I got out of bed and Marion says,

'What's that?'

I say, What?

She says, 'That,' and points.

I look down, Oh. An erection, I guess.

'Where'd that come from?' she says.

Don't know, I say, Maybe it's lost. Maybe it's looking for the young couple next door.

'Close the door,' says Marion.

I say, What?

'Finders, Keepers', she says. And I knew that was the last word.

Marion was an expert on last words. She had them catalogued inside her head, cross-referenced by levels of exasperation, mostly other people's, and they would hurt right deep down inside until you saw that corner of her mouth lift in a half-smile that said, *beat that*, and of course you couldn't, even if you knew where to begin. There was a time when I thought I'd like to have the last word but, the problem with last words is, they're so damn final they hang around forever.

You know, a man should be careful around wishes too. I remember once I wished so hard for the last word that I never heard it come around full circle until it took me from behind like a wolf and pulled me down here in this chair where it could gnaw at these old bones.

Especially on Sundays.

Sunday was such a good day. They began around nine a.m. with a dark coffee, fresh, not re-hashed from Saturday supper and two thin slices of evenly browned, evenly buttered toast. I never over-ate on Sundays, Marion always reminded me when I'd had enough and I can still touch my toes even though some days it might be easier if they were someone else's.

Marion said I should be grateful.

Perhaps I am.

She said I should be.

Perhaps I'll consider it.

'About time,' said Marion.

Later, I think.

'Always later,' said Marion.

And then I'd look over the car and swear I was going to trade it in for some old junk pile. The thing ran perfectly for years, apart from that one time with the rusted brake lines. And what use is a car like that on a Sunday? Marion said it was my fault. She said I'd spent so much of her housekeeping on that one special tool set and parts just waiting for it to break down that it would take one look at me with the cans and the boxes and the bright gleaming spanners and keep right on running 'cause it was afraid to do anything else.

She said the exhaust rattled when the engine stopped.

Sounds familiar, I said.

'Can't think why,' said Marion.

I'd go out to the front porch for the paper and the door has a hinge that's swollen with rust from the rain that strikes that particular corner on the days when it *should* rain, like Bank Holidays, and Easter and Christmas and New Year and from the days when it shouldn't like Mondays and Tuesdays when folk have to go about the business of just being and living and when you stop to think about it, it's hard enough having to work for a living without rain getting in the way.

I always thought rain should be saved for holidays, when there's time to go out and enjoy it for what it is and not hate it for what it stops you doing. Marion would say don't be so wet and I'd say it would be good to be able to plan for an umbrella and to know when to wear a coat. The hinge squeaks in the wind.

'Oil it,' says Marion.

I nod, That's what Sundays are for.

'It'll soon be Monday,' says Marion.

Oh, I'd say, looking at my watch, still fourteen hours twenty two minutes.

'Twenty one now,' says Marion.

Sunday evenings Marion played Bridge. I didn't. It took me forty years to unlearn Bridge to the point where I thought rubbers were something you wore on a Monday or a Tuesday in case it was raining. I'd take the hump for a walk instead. Seemed then like an arrangement that might last forever. Well, it seemed that way, until I learned that nothing lasts forever, I guess. Except, last words.

Marion made up the foursome with Hilda and George, and Henry, who owned the used Ford garage down by the supermarket. I worked at the garage for a time but Henry and I couldn't work it out any more then than when we were kids. Whenever I turned up for work he'd be outside pumping some fool's hand and lying like a trooper. I've seen folks slam the door and drive away leaving half of what they bought back there on the road in little brown flakes. I'd shake my head and he'd just shoo me away. I always bought Japanese.

I knew why Henry hated me then. I had Marion. He kept telling her how good they could be, how good they could be together, if only…

If only she didn't have me to look after, he meant. If only she didn't have to spend all of her time tidying up after me, the old man whose spark plug's sooted up and gone to that big scrapyard of the past and how the rest of me won't be too long behind it either. Me the fool, with a hump in the lawn that he won't put away and let go and who sits outside in the corner of the yard following the sun with his face like a big old sunflower and wishing for rain on Bank Holidays when he did his best trade and I swore one day when I hated Henry enough and it was sat inside me like an old kettle hissing and spitting away fit to turn me all sour and inside out, I'd let him have her.

She'd be back the next day.

I know.

She said so.

Henry dropped Marion off Sunday nights by the gate at about ten thirty. As she got out he'd lean across the seat and wave up at me. He knew I'd be there, watching him. He'd give Marion his most gleaming smile, all chrome and polish and second hand cars and somehow always manage to catch her by the elbow or the knee as she climbed out of his Porsche.

He'd shout, just so *I* could hear him.

'Night, Marion. Same time next week?

Damn fool asked that same question for fifteen years.

Marion says, 'Night, Henry… Around eight?

Henry would lean across to wind up the window, shout, 'See you then,' and drop the clutch.

He'd get about ten yards before Marion shouts,

Hey! Henry!

At that point, Henry would shed teeth into the bottom of the gearbox. He'd pull back the ten yards or so and wind down the window.

Marion says, 'Sorry, Henry…. It's not important…. It'll wait a week,' and drops the latch of the porch door behind her.

The hinge squeaks.

'Oil it, Frank,' says Marion.

Marion came through into the bedroom late one Sunday where I'm still stood at the window watching Henry's one good tail light weave along the roadwork's chicane down by the junction.

'He's a good man,' she says.

Yeah, perhaps I'll buy a car from him one day. It'll give me something to do Sundays while you're at Bridge.

'You need an interest,' says Marion.

Got one, I say.

Marion dodges around the bed.

'Had one,' she says.

Hilda still comes around on Tuesdays. Brings me all sorts of things I don't really need. Thankfully without George. Don't get me wrong, I don't mind George one little bit. What I object to is George with Hilda, attached by the hand like two schoolkids. Watching them does something to my insides. I once told Marion it's Hilda's way of making sure he didn't get lost and she said that's why she made a point of never holding mine. But you know, Hilda has one saving grace. It's that look in her eyes.

It's George, the damn fool.

The damn, lucky fool.

I felt the change come down with the leaves late that September, with them laid on the ground coppering the streets and the grass and the weeds by the hump slowing up and my time in the chair shortened to just a few minutes as the sun peeked over the gate and through the gap in the wall I'd made by throwing stones at the cats scurrying in the long grass.

I was out in the yard when the phone rang. Marion was sat in the lounge waiting for Henry to pip the horn of his little red Porsche and whisk her away to Hilda and George's and that other world from which I'd excluded myself all those years ago. To this day I don't know how, Marion never said a word I'll swear to that, but I heard everything that made her the way she was drop like a vase and shatter into bright, soundless pieces. I swear I heard her become silent. It rushed out through the door and into the yard and pushed me up out of the chair into the shade of the lounge where Marion sat with the lights out and the phone buzzing away in her hand and tears in her eyes and the voice of Hilda sounding tinny and lost as if she was stashed away at the back of all the tins in her cupboard.

I took the phone from Marion's hand.

Hilda? I'll call you back.

I sat down beside Marion and took her in my arms. Her eyes brimmed over against my cardigan, soaking the wool twists and through the holes into my shirt. I held her close and breathed the scent of her shampoo. One of Hilda's. She sobbed gracelessly, racking her breath against my chest and sniffing like nothing I ever heard since.....since myself when I made the hump.

It was Henry. They'd found his car spun around and broken all over the bottom of the west hill. He'd hit a car coming the other way head-on at the curve, out of control and at such a lick of speed that he never stood a chance.

Why would anyone like Henry fit rusty old Japanese brake lines to a '68 Porsche they said? It was way beyond them.

Marion seemed to go downhill for quite a while after that.

As we'd grown older, I found I never cared much about Henry one way or the other, at least, when he was alive. Oh, I'd watched him, knew what he wanted, but I always thought deep down that all I ever had to do was meet him at the porch one night and fasten my arm around Marion as she got out of the car and give him one of those looks and when he'd shout,

'See you next Sunday?'

I'd say, No, Henry, next Sunday we're going to the theatre.

Or maybe, We're having friends around.

Whatever it was, he'd know what I was really saying, but then come Sunday Marion would start to twitch and I'd begin to feel that what she really deserved was something more than one old man's jealousy and I'd begin to remember the sparkle in her eye, the way she came in from teasing Henry and I'd smile and probably offer to ring him myself and Marion would say,

'No, I'll do it, you'll only look a fool.'

And suddenly I'd realised that a look wouldn't be enough.

After Henry died, Sunday shifted its place in the week somehow. It became a day for wishing. A day for catching Marion unawares and forgetting and starting to get ready at seven o'clock still thinking in some dark recess of her mind that perhaps it was all a bad dream and Henry would roll up outside and the horn would sound, but then I'd watch as she'd mentally pinch herself before settling down again with the papers and a sigh like all her life being let out like a threadbare cat and no-one caring much if it came back in, except me, but somehow she never seemed to notice that.

Well, perhaps she was right, but how could I fight the past perfect, hiding back there in what was, where it can't make a mistake or mistime a punch aimed straight at your heart and through that to your head where it keeps bumping away and twisting things, lifting them up and elevating them out of proportion and I'd look at Marion's face and ask myself over again,

How do you kill a wish?

Should you ever wish to.

Weekdays Marion tried to talk to me and the words would spill down the old familiar rut into how she missed playing bridge on a Sunday and how if I tried, if I really tried, I could have learnt all over again but despite the words there was a silence inside her, as if a part of us had been walled off and the everydayness of her was lost somewhere far behind it in a place where I couldn't reach and the look on her face told me there was no use trying.

I began to lose touch with the hump. I used to spend my Sunday evenings sat in the chair in the corner of the yard by the grass and talk to it with my eyes closed and my memories wide open and we'd romp through January snow or Autumn-smelling woods with squirrels and birds, clattering at branches with a long stick and chasing acorns and chestnuts breaking smooth and moist under a late sun and some nights she'd be full grown and still a pup all at once and I'd watch with my minds eye as one grew into the other all over again and always with a stick in her mouth, but now Marion had this look about her that said she needed holding and talking to and when I did she'd just sit there quietly in my arms and tremble like the hump tracking rabbits along the burrows of its sleep until a tear would appear at the corner of her eye and she'd look at me and smile.

She'd shake her head and say,

Sorry, Frank.

Then she'd get up and go across to the window away from the sun and look out over the street to the side of town that was in shadow and watch the lights coming on street by street until the neon sign on top of the supermarket flickered into life and beside it, down behind the roofs and out of sight, there came the soft glow of lights from the car sales pitch. George and Hilda ran it then. Henry left it to them. It had the best parts store for a hundred miles.

They're so pretty, says Marion.

Yeah, it's the way they hold hands. I was on another track entirely.

They're so pretty, says Marion.

I put my hands on her shoulders, fall forward into the soft glow of moving lights,

Sorry, my love.

She never moves.

They're so pretty, says Marion.

I remember Hilda came around one Tuesday when it wasn't raining. Marion took her straight through into the bedroom as if her life depended on it.

A bare, 'Hello, Frank' scratched its way under the door and fell limp beside my chair out in the yard. I shouted back over my shoulder,

'Left hand thread barley sugar?'

Hilda had two of everything; canned, dried, preserved. George was still one of a kind, though he was looking a little wizened of late. Still, he wouldn't starve for a year. But all I heard was the soft clomp of the bedroom door behind them. I didn't worry, I knew she'd come out when she was ready and ask,

'Pink or Orange?' or maybe, 'How about a little tongue of bat, or eye of newt to give it a lift?'

When they finally did appear, they looked chastened, like kids caught smoking cigarettes that the older kids had bought and were now trying to hold all their insides in and not let it spill out on the ground where there's nothing to hide it.

Hilda said, 'We're going out, Frank. Won't be long. If you get a minute, ring George and tell him that behind the box of dried coriander on the top shelf there's a can or two of something he can heat up for his supper and not to worry about me, I'll be fine.'

They left. The air rushed in to fill the space like a thunderclap in my mind.

Marion hadn't spoken.

She came back alone around seven and went straight into the bedroom. I found her stood against the window. The first lights were beginning to show across in the east.

They're so pretty.

I felt her stiffen under my hands, but inside I could feel her crumple and fall until she was nothing but a husk, a shell planted rigid in a glass shore watching the electric tide wash in and over us until the room was dark and bursting with the rattle and hum of silences that I was afraid to break in case she fell apart under my hands and how, if she did, I could never fit all the pieces back, because, perhaps, I never knew how they really went, and now seemed a little late to be finding out when things like that take a lifetime, not just a few minutes in a darkened room.

She turned and placed a hand on my chest. Her eyes were hard and dry in the dark and for the first time since I remember they had no spark of humour, no light in the corners to show what was under the veil of what she said into the things she really meant.

You're not a bad man, Frank, said Marion.

I began to watch her almost out of the corner of my eye as if she were something that glanced off me and off of my life in a way that set us always moving but in different directions until we bounced back off Hilda or George, and times like that I was afraid to look at her because in her eyes I saw myself and the way she looked at me and saw that I wasn't a bad man.

Over a period she became leaner and sort of tired looking. I noticed her face and hands begin to fold and twist the way a photograph might when it's been thrown on the hot coals when it's not wanted, when the face on it no longer fits your life and perhaps to keep looking at it only makes you feel uncomfortable.

I saw all these things as if I was stood on a platform watching the trains go by, and every now and then I would recognise a face on one of them as Marion. Marion on a Monday, or a Tuesday when it was raining and as she got slow and wore that look of dark resignation, I'd look for her on a Sunday, and perhaps I'd find it in the edge of a smile as she watched the TV or sat with Hilda watching the lights and how each time that tide came in it pushed me further and further up the shore and away from all the pain in her face and every time I tried to stand still and look at it, it washed over me and flooded my brain with yesterdays and other, different Marions. I wasn't ignoring her pain but she wouldn't look and I just couldn't see.

After all, I'm not a *bad* man.

By the time the weather turned and the sun came high again across the yard Marion had grown kind of quiet and inwards as if she were thinking all the thoughts she knew how and making all of her decisions in a rush that spanned a lifetime.

She would sit in the kitchen with the phone limp in her hand and her eyes somewhere off far away and I'd come in from the yard and pick up the phone and listen to the sounds of Hilda rattling tins and pans in another kitchen three miles across town and I knew that she was only listening to the sounds that life makes when it's ordinary and vital like a yeast rising and not running away and rushing downhill to wind through darkness to oblivion like Henry's car and I could almost smell the nutmeg and cinnamon from where I stood and there would be a tear in Marion's eye and though it had no label and no loyalties, I knew it was for all that had been and not for the change that was coming.

That year was the first time the sun didn't clear the tops of the trees across the way. I knew that the trees had grown, but it felt in my heart like the sun itself had been weighted down as it passed across and watched us, me in the yard, Marion by the kitchen window where the light would catch her and ease the shivering and it seemed as though her illness had closed the door on summer, capturing something of winter right there inside her where fires and suns never reach, the kind of place, her face says, I've never been.

Later on that year George would take me to the hospital over the other side of town. We'd call in at home and Hilda would put food in front of me and I'd eat in a kind of slow motion, like a picture slowed down and played one frame at a time so that I could eke out this last time for as long as possible and how I wanted to get everything right and knew I couldn't do that at a rush but right behind me was Marion, pushing me forward into loss and loneliness as if she didn't care and couldn't wait to get there and ignoring all my wishes to stay and being determined to have the last word.

She begged them to let her home. She was hurting so much now she said it was all they could do and if they cared they'd let her be and let her be amongst the things she'd spent her life with, the things that knew about her and how to hold themselves just so when she tried to pick them up. She said that death was a stranger in any house, but if you had to let him in then a good fire and a soft chair that you knew would fit was no more than he'd come to expect. It always paid to be polite to company.

I remember, I picked her up and laid her into a warm salt bath. My eyes filled with tears as I released her and suddenly she was full again, the insistence of all those last words and teased arrogance pushing her skin out to where it used to be, before the world pushed it in and shredded it into the wrinkles under my hands. I dried my eyes, then dropped in the heater. After those first few moments I watched her soften and unfurl like a dry autumn leaf in a clear pool. She'd opened her eyes and floated free and away from me and the look in them said forever, *'I know, Frank, you're not a* bad *man.'*

She'd known, that day. I'd had to make her know. I'd held her hand and wished I could say all those things that you think of at odd times, like when you're in the shower, or the sound of a sports car scratches an itch from out of the past and the feeling sort of floods through you and you think, the very next time I'm going to say that, and when I do she'll *have* to understand, and even after all this time she'll know that it never went away but somewhere along it just sort of glanced off and became dislodged into a place around a corner out of sight, but my eyes filled and my throat became solid like the bole of an old gnarled wishing-tree and all I could do was make choking sounds and shake my head from side to side as the tears ran into my mouth and filled it with the taste of bitterness.

She'd looked up at me and said,

I know, Frank, I know.

You're not a bad man.

The garden needs weeding. The borders are frayed like these here cuffs.

Hey, Marion?

Oh well, she would've been home soon. And when she came it'd be…

Frank, look at this, and Frank, look at that, and where should it be and why do I bother?

…then the door would slam and she'd be gone again until who knows when and then just like the tide she'd storm back up the beach and rattle and push at the shingle of my thoughts and bits of possessions scattered around just the way I liked 'em and, for God's sake, why shouldn't I?

Oh… I don't know, where was I?

The weeds.

Oh yes. The weeds. They've run amok. Especially the corner by the azaleas where it looks as though the cats have been burying or scurrying or something.

Where's the strimmer?

I suppose Marion would know.

Come on Frank! You were doing something only last Tuesday, or was it Thursday...

Oh what the hell, nothing seems to matter anymore since Marion... ah, there it is!

No plug!

Come on Frank, where's the plug?

On the heater.

Where's the heater?

In the bathroom.

Still?

Marion would have known.

The hump looks larger now the weeds have been cut down. I can sit here and throw stones at the cats or I can go back inside until the sun hits this spot by the chair again tomorrow. It doesn't seem right to go about moving the chair after it's been in this place for so long.

I would hate it to resent me.

I look over to the hump and I remember how it used to be still sometimes, and not even let you know that it was listening until you moved one foot out of place, and how just under its surface ran something wilder and hot through its veins that even now pushes up through the soil and grows weeds like a body has never seen and it held all that closed like a flower just so that we could be together and when it thought no-one was looking it would share it with me and show it to me in all those little ways with sticks and smells and looks and most of all I wish Marion would come back now and she'd say,

'What are you doing by that fool dog's grave again when the rest of the garden's gone to hell, and if you'd really cared you'd never have let me talk you into putting it down in the first place. Would you?'

And I'd say,

Hey, Marion, don't shout at me, I'm not a bad man.

Just look at the time.
She'd have been here real soon.
You'd maybe have given her another minute or two, that's all.
Or listened out for my brothers' car, if it was Sunday.
It was a Porsche.
You couldn't miss it.

A Twist of Glass

I didn't think too much about this story after I had written it. In fact, it hid amongst the dross on my computer for years before I took it out and read it again. Then it made me cry. (No, it's not *that* bad, I'm just a soppy old sod.)

It's a story about all the daftness that surrounds young love... the myths that we grow up with from the playground about how it will be and all our dreams of finding that perfect someone and how they will fill our lives to capacity and love will thrum our hearts like the strings on a double bass.

All true. And it all happens. But none of it is as good as the anticipation of seeing that one truly undeniable sign that this is the one... that this person is the culmination of your teenage hopes and dreams... or as devastating as the worry that you are not going to be strong enough to deal with it.

Thomas needn't have worried. What he'd found that day in the Post Office was nothing short of perfection... and she would be strong enough for both of them...

A Twist of Glass

'It's not glass,' said Thomas.

Eliza reached out a finger to stroke the curved flank, 'It's cold!'

Thomas watched the wonder in her smile, 'It's a real'un.'

'Don't be silly.'

'I tell you. It's a real'un.'

Eliza remained staring into the cold, translucent fire of the horse, 'It's crystal.'

Thomas reached out and touched it's tiny head, then smiled a quiet, secretive smile, 'As much you know.'

Eliza looked at him then slowly returned her gaze to the horse, her eyes lit from within by a pale glow, 'He's beautiful!'

Thomas pushed his hands into his pockets and shook his head.

Eliza laughed once softly, almost a sob, 'What's the matter?'

'What do *you* know?' asked Thomas, 'Can't you see?'

Eliza looked at him sharply, 'See what?'

'It's not a 'He'.'

Eliza turned back to the display where the crystal horse reared, the glass shelf spinning it slowly and majestically in the centre of the shop floor.

Thomas pointed as it came back around towards them, 'Look! There. There's nothing'.'

His face suddenly flushed, 'See. I told yer.'

Eliza stroked the smooth underbelly with the back of a slim knuckle, 'It's not a 'She' either.'

'I know,' said Thomas, his eyes full of answers, his expression as if he had caught the tail of something and was afraid to let go, 'It's a... no, it's a nothing.'

'It's not a 'nothing',' said Eliza, 'It's beautiful.'

'Yes, I know,' said Thomas, the flush of his skin deepening, 'It is. I mean, it's beautiful.' His words tumbled out in a sudden rush, '...but it's more than that, it's...'

He hesitated, attempting to gauge the look on her face, the wonder in her eyes as she watched the horse slowly spinning.

'It's... look,' he said, and took her slender forefinger and pressed it gently against the horses forehead.

'Tell me what you feel.'

'It's crystal,' said Eliza.

'Is that all?' Thomas looked at her strangely, as a dark indecision crossed his face.

'It's smooth,' said Eliza, never taking her eyes from the horse, '...and quite, quite, beautiful.'

Thomas turned away for a moment and seemed to be struggling with something that tore him this way and then another, as if a tide were at work within him.

'I'll buy it you,' he said.

Eliza stared impassively at him, 'It's too much money.'

Thomas clung hard to his decision, 'I will. I'll buy it you.'

Eliza looked again at the horse, the corners of her mouth lifting slowly into a half smile. She winked secretly at it.

'What's the favour then?'

'Your Mom and Dad's away for't weekend.'

Eliza laughed once, softly, then nodded.

Thomas's head lay warm and moist between Eliza's breasts. A tear flowed softly along the bridge of his nose and across her skin to collect in the dimple just below her shoulder. She held him to her with a gentle, quiet strength she'd always hoped she would find.

Thomas snuffled, 'I'm sorry,' he said. His breath and words tickled her skin as they lay entwined.

Eliza splayed her fingers around the arc of his shoulder blade, stroking him reassuringly, 'Don't be sorry. Another day, another time. When it's right for both of us.'

Thomas shifted slightly. The small pool of tears emptied cold across Eliza's shoulder and into the bedding.

'You must think I'm daft,' he said.

Eliza turned her attention to the tousled auburn hair behind his ear, drawing it into whirls with her finger, 'Why must I think that?'

'Well, *I* think I'm daft.'

'That's no good reason.'

Thomas lifted his head to look at the horse. Eliza drew him gently back into her embrace.

'It is,' he said. 'You can be daft, you know, just for a minute and then be all right again, as if nothing were ever the matter.'

'I don't know,' said Eliza, 'Although perhaps I do. I remember that first time I saw you at the post office.'

They laughed together.

'Perhaps even for longer than a minute,' she said.

They lay together for a while, frozen in space like the horse that watched them from the dresser.

'Have you ever believed in somethin',' asked Thomas, '...somethin' you know to be daft, somethin' that would make other people think you were daft, and you still believed in it anyway?'

'Like God, you mean?'

'No,' said Thomas, 'Not like God. Nearly everybody believes in God, or somethin' like it anyway. No, somethin' strange. Somethin' like you thought you'd never see and then just for a minute you thought you did.'

He shook his head, 'I thought *I* did. I was wrong. I'm sorry.'

'There's no reason to be sorry.'

'There *is*.'

Eliza lifted his head so that she could see his face in the gentle glow, 'I told you, another day, another time. When it's right for *us*.'

Thomas's expression closed in upon itself, 'It's not that.' He buried his head in shame, 'I'm sorry for the things I thought, the way I felt.'

A tremor ran through him, 'The things I thought I saw, they made me think that, perhaps, this might be easy. You might be...'

She hugged him tightly to her, 'Tell me then. Tell me what you thought you saw. You're not daft. A belief isn't something to be ashamed of, however simple it might be.'

When Thomas spoke, his voice seemed distant and somehow, much younger, 'The horse,' he said, 'It was the horse.'

He fell silent then.

'Yes?' said Eliza.

'It wasn't,' said Thomas, 'A horse, I mean. Just for a moment...'

'Yes?' said Eliza.

'Just for a moment...' said Thomas. He lifted his head and looked up at her, 'What do you know about... Unicorns?'

Eliza smiled, 'Something,' she said, 'A little.'

'When I was a kid,' said Thomas, 'I read every book I could find about them. Read every story that had one in it. I knew them almost by heart, and as I grew up it seems to have stayed there deep down inside of me, you know, this belief that somewhere there might be one and that some day I might just see...'

Eliza smoothed his hair, 'And you thought that, yesterday, you'd found one. Is that it?'

Thomas thought for a moment, 'Maybe I did. I don't know.'

'How would you tell?'

Thomas shuffled around to where he could see the horse poised on the dresser,

'Well,' he said, 'They say that Unicorns only appear to someone who's a virgin and pure in thought...' he blushed as he realised the implications of this admission, '...and when I first saw it I could have sworn it had a horn on its forehead, a beautiful twisted thing with a spiral all around it, and I would have staked my life that its eyes shone like gold and watched me and followed me as it turned around.'

'What a beautiful thing to believe in,' said Eliza. She touched him on the forehead and rubbed him gently where the nub of a horn might be.

'It was so *real*,' said Thomas, 'As real as a dream when you're in it. I honestly thought it was real.'

'But that's beautiful,' said Eliza, 'Beauty shouldn't make you sorry.'

'I'm not sorry I saw it, or even that I thought I saw it. I'm glad. It was as if I'd waited all my life for just that minute. But when I knew that you couldn't see it, it made me look at you in a different way. I thought, if you were like I always thought you were, then you'd be able to see it too. Then when you couldn't, I thought that perhaps you might... if I bought you the horse, then maybe I could talk you into... you know, and then when I looked back it had gone. And I looked and I looked but it was just a crystal horse and there was no horn and no spiral and its eyes were just clear glass and they wouldn't look at me anymore.'

Eliza stroked his head back down upon her chest.

'Don't be sorry. You found your Unicorn. Perhaps most people never do. Maybe people believe all their lives without ever really knowing.'

She turned out the light and gazed across the room to the dresser, to where the beautiful golden eyes gazed back at her and a pale horn twisted the night about its spiral.

A Settling of Dust

…is a story of obsession and self-delusion brought on by grief.

My father was one of those unlucky people fated to die an early death. A curious fact surrounding death in any immediate family is that the level of shared grief at the passing seems inversely proportionate to the remaining life-span they could otherwise have expected, and the effect this has on the bereaved after an untimely death, (my own father was 42 years of age), can therefore be profound.

For myself it began a process where, internally, I underwent an emotional acceleration while, externally, I was cold as stone, and I must say, somewhat erratic. I did and said things without thinking because my thought patterns were so fast that they skipped over the loss of a parent quickly, so that I didn't have to see it. The rest of my movements were that of an automaton, and about as moral, as aesthetically responsible and as inexplicable as those of that same robot.

For my mother, it began a degenerative process of non-acceptance of the fact that she had a life remaining. In some things she became obsessive, hiding behind anti-depressants and subjugating her emotions in hard work while I spun indecisive internal circles like a top.

In retrospect, my heart goes out to her and I wish she could now see the man I eventually turned out to be but, sadly, she herself died at 63, after just three and a half years of a deserved retirement by the sea, convinced that she would find heaven in the waiting arms of my father.

For all who knew me in those turbulent moments, I offer an apology.

A Settling of Dust

The corner in which the party sat, sequestered by short chromium posts, slung between with thick, white, fraying ropes, seemed unnaturally quiet. Emily wondered if this arrangement was to protect them from the curious, or to protect the curious from the grief within. All it needed was a sign that said,

Reserved for The Wake.

The Co-op was busy. Unusually so, but on a cold day such as today, thought Emily, there'd be no sandwiches in the park and no sun to warm your back, and now no other back to warm. No Albert to snuggle up to. To put your arm around. To tip a lazy leg over and between to feel the soft hairs slide against your own skin.

She quenched the rising spark of a tear with pale, tepid tea from an over-delicate china cup. The restaurant clattered its bleak, oblong length back at her, echoing the teaspoons of elderly couples seated across from each other over scones and dark, damson jams, staring blankly and wide-eyed with that look of everything having already been said at breakfast.

She opened her eyes, which had never been closed, and smiled. *That would never happen now, for her. Perhaps it's time for a new start.* For all of us, she thought. She felt a large moss-less stone of emotion begin to roll inside her, and knew she couldn't stop it. Her sister's hand tightened around her arm.

She patted the gloved fingers gently, *'I'll be alright.'*

She watched idly as her sister attempted to remove a tea cup handle from her delicately gloved finger. *Some things don't change,* thought Emily. Young Billy for another. She watched him titivating his tie and ogling the waitress. She, poor, pert thing, with good legs and a pleasant though desperate face, was pretending not to see. Eunice looked up, once.

Eunice sat across the table from her, silently scouring the sand-coloured servers for wisps of forlorn lettuce and wet, flatfish dabs of tomato.

God knows what Billy sees in her, thought Emily. She seemed squat and withdrawn, like a barrel fermenting quietly in the corner waiting for someone to tap it. It wouldn't be Billy, Emily could see that now as his admiring eyes followed the waitress around the table.

She raised a finger to the waitress, then, as the stone rolled hard and implacable inside her, held her cup to the wrong side. The waitress bent far over the table. Billy's eyes stood out like chapel hat pegs. He looked up to find Emily smiling at him.

She'd knock the dust off you, thought Emily.

Eunice sifted the bits of flake that had drifted on the current from the gateau and watched in silence.

'Wait here, Sis,' said Alice, once they'd reached the pavement outside, 'I'll get Derek to fetch the car around.'

She grabbed Billy, who'd been the last to leave and who now quickly trammelled the bottom few steps trying not to look as if he was catching up.

'If anybody tries to park, see 'em off will you?'

'Alright, Mom.'

'No,' said Emily, surprised at the sudden firmness in her own voice, and the crushing force of the unstoppable stone she could feel rolling inside her, 'I'll catch the bus.'

'Don't be silly,' said Alice, 'Do as you're told for once. Derek's already gone for the car. We have to go that way. It's no trouble. And even if it was, it's Albert's funeral. He'd have wanted it.'

'How would *you* know?' asked Emily, as the stone crashed and tumbled thunderously inside her.

'Well...'

'Well... exactly,' said Emily. 'Here, Billy. I forgot to tip the waitress.'

She took a five pound note from her bag and held it out, 'Would you mind?'

Billy smiled, straightened his tie, then took the stairs two at a time.

'Alice,' said Emily, taking her arm. She pulled her away from the edge of the road, 'How long is it since Albert and I got into a car with you and Derek?'

'Don't know,' said Alice, trying to peer amongst the traffic for the arrival of a pale puce hatchback, 'Can't remember. Is it important, *now*?'

'It wasn't me that wouldn't get in. It was Albert. Said he wouldn't ride with a hypocrite.'

'Emily!'

Emily smiled. Alice's face was a grotesquery of mirrors and emotions. She wrung her hands together. The tight black leather gloves squeaked in protest.

'Emily! How could you. Derek has never, ever, said a wrong word. Not to you nor Albert. Not ever.'

God, how static this family has become, thought Emily. The stone inside her shook and rumbled impatiently. *It needs grabbing by the tail feathers and the dust shaking out.*

A pale puce hatchback drew up alongside them. The door slung open and Emily pushed her open-mouthed sister into the front, 'He didn't mean Derek.'

Alice's mouth remained the perfect oval.

'He knew about your boyfriend,' said Emily.

She nodded at Derek, who smiled wanly back, unsure of just what was happening.

'You can tell *him* it's a cleaning job. But Albert knew better. And so does half the street.'

She closed the door. The car drew a few feet up the road and stopped, suddenly. Emily turned away towards the bus stop as Billy came hurrying down the stairs, his face flushed and bright. Emily kissed Eunice once, and very publicly, on the cheek, 'Bye, kids.'

'Bye, Auntie.' Billy gave her hand an extra squeeze. Eunice allowed herself to be led away towards the car park. When the bus arrived, the first thing Emily noticed was how filthy it was inside. She scratched distractedly at a mark on the seat until she almost missed her stop.

Next morning, Emily awoke, dressed, and went downstairs. Entering the lower part of the house, she felt crushed by the tension of its held breath. She moved from room to room opening curtains and windows, allowing it to exhale it's quiet pressure onto the street until the rooms hung with the scent of silence from the pale, wallpaper flowers.

When the house is quiet like this, she thought, *time seems to become elastic.* She felt it stretch around her then, encompassing the day and all the little things that needed attention. The things Albert had made her leave alone.

No, he'd say, *It belongs there. Give it peace, woman.* Well, he had all the peace he wanted, now.

He was right though, thought Emily, *there are things in life that will remain forever in the same place, doing nothing. Until something pushes.*

At one p.m., she turned on the radio to listen to the early news. On a sudden impulse, she pulled a duster from the drawer and rubbed the old pencil mark from the dial.

Suddenly, the radio blared in something European, French maybe. Inexplicably, the voice filled the room with its change and made the stone inside her move again, charging her with its growing, insistent motion. She picked up the tea pot and lifted the lid. Inside, it was brown and deeply ingrained. It seemed an age before the scourer made any impact at all.

At one thirty she moved across the kitchen, idly spinning the radio dial. Static hissed back at her from the shelf where it glared like a cornered serpent. She advanced slowly towards it, duster held in front. She flicked at the dial. Piano. Albert hated piano. She turned it up. She pulled out a chair and sat down to eat toast. The tea was cold. When she'd turned on the grill, she'd noticed the marks on the cooker top. And the knobs had been dirty. Ingrained. *Static. Needing a push.* The soda was good but it wrinkled her skin like a monkey's.

Finishing the toast she washed the plate and the tea cup in the sink. The cup had a brown ring in the bottom, in the corner between the side and the flat bit.

The rest of the tea service seemed to be the same.

By the time she had worked her way through into the living room, leaving behind kitchen cupboards neatly packed, their shelves covered in fresh, stiff sheets of greaseproof paper, and sell-by dates calendared in precise rows, all the cups, plates and jugs had been stacked or, if cracked and chipped, thrown away.

On the corner of the sideboard nearest the door, the telephone sat in patient silence. Emily eyed it watchfully, then picked up Albert's darts trophy that was the furthest thing from it she could find. She dusted it, wiping with great effort and concentration down amongst the crevices and folds of the ludicrously slim and athletic figure of the player.

She dusted the shelf beneath it and replaced it hurriedly in case the phone rang. The phone remained patiently silent. Emily watched it from the far corner. She listened to the silence and heard it not ringing with the great clarity and concentration that comes from a total awareness of the instrument and its capacity.

We're sorry, it had said the week before, *We're sorry, Mrs Derry.* It had even known her name, but then it had her number too, *We're very sorry, Mrs Derry, but Albert's been taken ill, and, well... we're very sorry, Mrs Derry.*

Emily had never considered the possibility of a telephone as *we.* But then, she only ever noticed the one, and out there, beyond this watchful silence there must be, what? A million of them? And all of them sorry, no, not *sorry...* but... *Very, very, sorry, Mrs Derry.*

Slowly and quietly, she got down to her hands and knees. Keeping her head below the level of the sideboard top, she crawled to the cable connected to so much sorrow and snapped it from the socket. The phone glared in sorry impotence from its bland, grey cradle. Daring now, she reached up and took it. First she wiped the dial, and the little places where the plastic bar slid in and out, blowing into the crevices to flush out the dust of grief hiding in there and waiting so she would carry it to her ear where it could filter in and whisper to her in the darkness and the coldness and the lack.

She wiped the mouthpiece so that her next words would transmit themselves fresh and unattached with things of the past, so that all things previously said could be forgotten and laid down in the dust. With Albert. *And Albert.* His mouth had been here. He had spoken words. Where were they? She looked down into the mesh, hoping to find something that her moment's thoughtlessness had missed. But they had gone. She might have saved something. A last goodbye. Or a wrong number. But no, they were gone. *Moved.*

She wiped the space beneath the silent telephone and replaced it, two inches to the left. No sooner had it left her fingers than it rang, once. The sound hung in the air until Emily wondered if she had heard it at all. She picked it up. Silence. And in the background, static. Emily stared at the unplugged cable while free electrons danced, bubbled and hissed sinuously in her ear.

'*How could you?*' said the voice of Alice. The static hissed between her words like the fall of a million tears drenching a forest and dripping effortlessly through the leaves.

'*How could you?*'

Emily breathed slowly into the mouthpiece, filling the freshly cleaned space with her breath, with her present, displacing all the pasts there might have been. The words came then, fresh, unsullied, free of all attachment,

'I'm sorry. Something… something moved. Inside me. And I can't… I can't.'

Slowly, she replaced the receiver.

Getting to her feet, more angry now than afraid, she went into the kitchen and returned with a large pair of scissors and cut the plug from the end of the phone wire. She picked up the handset. Silence. Total and absolute. She replaced it quietly on its cradle.

It rang again.

'*How could you?*' said Eunice. The static hiss scratched Emily's ear with the sound of finger nails scrabbling at plates for those tiny extra crumbs of comfort.

'*How could you?*'

'It was... time,' said Emily, striving for newness, now that sorrow had become second-hand. 'You were taking up time.'

She replaced the receiver once more, 'And there's never enough.'

She turned slowly... and saw for the first time the dust that covered the whole of the room.

The German silver fruit bowl with its black inlay caught and burnished in the dusty light as Emily replaced it by the phone. She picked up the gilt picture frame next and wiped the space beneath it before sitting down to pick at the moulding and curlicues with the corner of a cloth. Albert smiled up at her. Static, now. Immobile, immoveable, his face loomed at her from the depths of this gold-fringed abyss and tried to suck her downwards into the past. She put it down quickly, brushed her hand against the telephone.

We're very sorry, Mrs Derry... Mrs Derry?... Mrs Derry?

She opened the top drawer and began to polish the playing cards in their smart plastic pack, then the table lighter, the corkscrew, the front edge of the drawer, and all the time moving the dust further and further back, pushing it behind her and moving on, rolling with the huge boulder inside her, nudging it aside.

The dried flower arrangement was proving difficult. The dust clung to every petal and leaf where Albert's old toothbrush couldn't dislodge it. Emily filled the sink and left them to soak. She picked up the clock. It was ten to eight. No wonder she was light-headed. She took three slices of bread from the cabinet and buttered them both sides to minimise the risk of crumbs. She rolled them together and held herself rigidly over the waste bin as she forced them into her mouth and down her throat against the sense of time rising from within her, regurgitating the past and reminding her of all the things she knew were attracting the dust. She gagged on the bread but managed to hold it down. She took out the waste bag with its few crumbs and folded it neatly into the bin in the yard. At the doorstep she took off her shoes in case they carried in the smell and taste of the outside. Without thinking, she removed her tights. She lifted the hem of her dress. It smelled strongly of dust.

Emily returned to the clock and polished the ship-wheel case, the brass cold against her naked skin as she clutched it tightly to her. She wiped the top of the cabinet and slid the clock back into place. A plastic doily slipped off the newly polished surface and disappeared down the back. Laid full-length across the carpet, Emily peered under the cabinet. Along the top edge of the skirting board the dust sat, waiting. She was horrified. How long had it been there, just... waiting?

She fetched the vacuum from the kitchen cupboard where it hid, shining and freshly buffed. She connected the hoses and attachments and reached beneath the cabinet just as the phone rang.

It rang once. It wouldn't ring again. It knew she had heard. She could tell by its air of calm indifference as it sat on the sideboard daring her to ignore it. Teasing her to want to know. To share in its grief-laden torrent of useless, redundant, second-hand words of no-comfort. Emily reached over and lifted the receiver.

It was Billy. She knew it was Billy. The hiss hugged itself to her, covering her skin with its soft sibilance and in the background was the sound of Billy breathing hard. Billy just run down the steps. Billy just run up the steps. Billy laid out round and fat across some poor, pert waitress and her good legs wrapped around him and him overlapping her, spilling over onto the floor and the thing he was giving her taking the desperation from her face only to put it back later when all the dust had settled... and Billy breathing hard and blowing that dust around... she breathing it in through her dark stockings and white cap and apron and opened mouth gasping *thank you thank you thank you* in the dusty musty air and then... only static. Hiss. Hiss. Hiss. But it was Billy. She *knew* it was Billy.

She put down the phone.

No, Billy. Not thank you... not for this.

As the hissing stopped, the vacuum began.

The carpet heaved beneath the pull of the cleaner. Its fibres sprang upright in the suction of air and the friction of dust. Emily pushed the tube hungrily into all the dark corners. Into places she may have missed before, or places where the dust had whispered to her, convincing her that they were empty and clean and didn't need touching. The places where the dust had sat in the darkness, quietly breeding; unseen and unsuspected and waiting for her to become distracted; to take her eye off the ball and here it came now tumbling out and covering everything and erasing all the changes.

Emily knew why it was here. It had come to try to convince her that change was futile. If something moved, you could perhaps see for a time where it had once been. Until the dust settled again and made it look as if it had always been that way and as though a change had never taken place. She understood now why Albert had believed that some things should never move. That way the dust can't obliterate the changes. But Emily was ready for a fight.

She stubbed the tube into the space behind the television. The vacuum lifted a corner of the rug. Beneath it, a line of dust sat complacent and contemplative around the edge.

Emily began to move the furniture.

As she shifted one end of the sideboard, the phone rang. Emily cut the wire to the exchange that came in through the hole drilled in the corner of the window, then snipped the wire that connected the receiver to the cradle and ignored it.

The phone in the hall rang. Once.

'*How could you?*' said Derek.

The static whined plaintively, implacable in its similarity of tone and in the background was the sound of hearts awakening and eyes snapping open like roller shutters on market day and all things laid out bare and inescapable and carrying a terrible price. '*How could you?*'

'I thought I could afford it,' said Emily,' I thought I had the time. But the dust… you see. It couldn't wait.' And from within the static came the sound of glass illusions breaking.

She put the phone back on the hook. Looking down, she noticed the edge of the stair board where the line of dust rode upwards, unperturbed in its conquest of the stairs.

Emily slid finally into bed between crisp, white sheets freshly spread, ironed and smoothed into place. The soft pillow case beneath her head took the dust from her hair and from the places where it had hidden ingrained in the folds of her skin.

Around her, the house shone like a monumental beacon to change. The windows were cleaned, fastened and locked. In all the rooms the furniture had been re-arranged, scratches stained and re-polished, carpets vacuumed and shampooed, curtains washed and the bulbs changed in the light fittings. In the garage, Albert's old car shone like a showroom demagogue.

She slipped exhausted into the cool of the sheets, wondering idly what she would do with the rest of her life.

On the table beside the bed, the castrated telephone rang. Once.

Without thinking, in that half-way house between sleep and frustration, she picked it up.

'*How could you?*' said Albert. In her ear the hiss of static pulsed with the beat of a million discordant hearts in perpetual motion, '*How could you?*'

Emily smashed the handset against the wall. Wires sprang from the cheap plastic casing. Bits of it showered the newly cleaned floor beside the bed. Emily leapt from the sheets to pick them up. Microphones and speakers dangled puppet-like from tiny circuit boards that crushed easily between her fingers.

'*We're sorry, Mrs Derry,*' they said, '*We're very, very sorry.*'

And in every room, from where it had floated unnoticed and silently pressed against the ceiling by the heat rising from the now cooled radiators, the dust began to settle.

The Big Idea

Here is where we come back to one of my favourite themes... being seven.

One day, in Loutro on the sunny isle of Crete, I attended a workshop run by Bernadine Evaristo, a wonderful short fiction writer in her own right (write?)

The purpose of the exercise was to consider what we would say to our younger self if we could travel back in time.

Would we warn him/her about the girl/boy who would founder their teenage ship on the rocks? Would we give them financial advice? What indeed would we, or should we, warn them of.

I considered this for a while then began to write with the premise that if I went back with advice, and it was heeded, then perhaps I would not be sat here in the glorious sunshine considering this problem. I could be anywhere, in prison even!

Or I could have ceased to exist altogether.

Whatever transpired, I would not be me, and being me is not necessarily an unhappy thing. It has benefits, although I've not always been aware of them, and this project made me think harder than usual. I came up with a different solution. I began to look at the things we lose as we get older, acuity of thought and vision, the tempering of our expectations and the ability to think outside the box with that freshness of eye that comes with being seven.

So... instead of giving him something... I decided to borrow that eye...

The Big Idea

'Do I know you, mester?'

No, but you will

I watch his face twist with slow bewilderment. He turns around quickly, this way and that, never losing me from the corner of his eye.

'Where did you come from?'

I smile at the quiff his mother lovingly raises every morning. I see in the mirror the dark hair spilling out between her fingers, tucked by the comb. A quiet musty smell pervades his clothes and skin and I guess that here, now, it must be Thursday.

That doesn't matter

'Everybody comes from somewhere.'

I remember the check of the shirt he is wearing, know well how the blues and the greens would feel against my skin, the soft flannel of the short grey trousers with the hard ridge of doubled seam that I know is chiding his leg, making his crotch sore.

He shifts from foot to foot, rocking purposefully in the sunlight that spills into the yard from the lips of three-storey terraces, steaming attics crumpled with stale beds beneath glass-lights fastened shut to keep out a sudden rain.

Billy...

I register the slight shock that displaces the perennial smile.

Go... to the toilet

He hops, undecided, then streaks for the familiar door, third along the block with its neatly cropped pages of 'The Sheffield Star' pegged behind on a rusty nail.

While I wait I realise that I can't easily tell him how I know these things, or how to prepare himself for me. He returns amidst the sound of falling water and plants his feet square, slightly apart, in anticipation of the breadth of frame he will one day have. I reach out to touch the short sleeve of his shirt, checking my own memories, testing my age for symptoms. He steps away backwards.

Tell me a secret

He wonders, still smiling, guessing how deep he dare pass into the stream that runs beneath small boys where they sit on causeway edges, dangling their fresh imaginations into that flashing, caustic, dangerous fancy.

'Last Friday,' he says, coming closer with a shadowed, sideways twist, 'You won't tell my mom I telled you, will you, mester?'

Despite myself, and him, I let out a short, bitter laugh. The crumbling ochre brick and the stone-silent windows of the yard push it back at me.

I promise

He scuffs his feet, his gaze falling abjectly on the bared leather toes, the brogues with the too high sides that are irritating the scabs on his heel bones, the laces he has just worked out how to tie.

'Last Friday,' he says, '…my dad set fire to the chimney.'

I try hard to look surprised, but fail.

Is that your best secret?

He squints slyly at me, then spins on one foot, always out of reach.

'No.'

Then what is?

'It's *my* best secret.'

What is?

'If I telled you then it wouldn't be.'

Do you tell your mom your secrets?

He shrugs, but I already know the answer.

His socks dishevel themselves heedlessly around his ankles, one three inches higher than the other, flagging up even now, at seven, the impending imbalance in his soul.

'Where *did* you come from, mester?'

He searches my face for things he might recognise.

What's more important, is where you're going to

I know that will be cryptic enough to trigger in him that lapsing, but insatiable curiosity.

'I can't go anywhere.' His toe stubs the concrete, a temporary, rolling hopelessness chastening his voice, 'My mom says.'

Where would you want to go?

I perch myself on the lid of a steel dustbin. He dances out of reach smartly, eyes left, then right, displaying an awareness that will soon restrict him to seek security above all else, colouring his life with the checks of his shirt, the thin red line of small successes, the blue of impending sadness, the green of the insidious jealousies that will fade but never wash clean in the 'Reckits Blue' of his circumstance.

'I don't know,' he says, with a petulance as though I'd expected him to fall fully-formed and complete at my feet, 'Not yet.'

What if you never know?

'My mom says I will. She says…' and he slides his face up to the sun, where the slicing light touches and frames the memory of her words.

We speak them together.

'She says I'm full of Big Ideas.'

He stops, his smile for once frozen and impenetrable.

'What *are* you, mester?'

I think for a moment, then smile openly at my ability to retreat at will through the downward years.

I'm a Big Idea

He warms again at that, and I see the wall behind his eyes erode.

'I'm not scared.'

Should you be?

He pushes his hands deep into his pockets, withdraws the sea shell I know is there, turns it in his fingers, plunging one into the small pink ear before returning it to the pocket without the hole.

'Perhaps.'

Why should you be scared of an idea?

'Mom says mine will always get me into trouble.'

Hmm

I nod in agreement, watching him watching me.

'Will you get me into trouble, mester?'

Lots of it. And with a lot of people. But you'll survive

'Your eyes…' he says, 'They're the same as my moms. But your hair is silver… like my Granddad's. Does that mean you're old?'

He takes a step closer, leans in towards me as far as he dare. I back away a step.

'Do you know my mom?'

Yes

'Shall I fetch her?'

No…

How can I see her young again, knowing she will always be? Something inside me tears open and I drop through, a sensation of rope around my throat, a pressure of fluid hot behind my eyes.

No. I'm not ready to meet your mom. Not yet. Please don't tell her I was here. It can be our best secret

He looks me up and down, the faded jeans and the white tee shirt flagging up something for his attention.

'Are you a sailor?'

I think about that for a moment, the way I've arrived, the peculiar iridescent sea I've had to sail.

Yes

His eyes widen at the sight of my white deck shoes with no laces. I speak quickly then, before he takes me further down a road I am unprepared to travel.

So tell me your next-best secret

He looks around the yard furtively, then lowers his face into shade, his eyes becoming dark empty pools, his mouth small and quiet with shadow.

'…you wouldn't like me if I telled you.'

I would…

'…You won't, honest, mester.'

I always will…

'…promise?'

And more…

'I… I killed something.'

A chill of memory streaks through me until its fist of ice clamps around my heart. How can I have forgotten the sparrow? Fragile and fleeting, a grace note struck from the melody of the sky.

No. You haven't

'Yes I have. Grandma says so.'

I lean forward to see if I can catch the haunting of his eye, the sad corner of his mouth. He tips his head further down.

'Mom found a sparrow on the floor yesterday morning.'

I remember the way the sparrows used to flock around the yard by the hundred, chirruping the ridge tiles, swooping to the weeds pushing their way through the edges of the concrete, stealing caterpillars and greenfly, scouring the rough surfaces with their beaks for breadcrumbs snapped from the tablecloth, and how they would sometimes fall from the sky like discarded pieces of memory, dislodged ideas.

Was it hurt?

Watching his shame I can sense how far apart we are. Far more than fifty years and a gulf of experience. Far more than a faulty memory. Less, but far more than a stranger, I realise how little he is learning to love himself, and I love him all the more for it now...

'It was flapping around and couldn't stand up. Mom picked it up and put it in there.'

He points to the milk-box on the wall beside the back door, a bit of stained rough ply big enough to hold four pints, a nailed-on sloping roof that lifts up to put the bottles in.

'Dad put a bit of wire in front so it couldn't get out until it was better. Mom let me give it some bread crumbs and some milk in a eggcup.'

Did it get better?

'No...'

And that was your fault?

He looks up at me then as if I won't believe him unless I can see the way it has marked his face, realigned the directness of his gaze, held shut some as yet unopened flower.

'Grandma says it was. Me and Mick...'

Wiggy?

I see immediately Mick's plump-faced smile beaming out from under a blue and grey school cap.

'...we were going round the yard on our scooters, pretending to be fire engines like the one that came to see to the chimney. We were shouting and dinging like bells and Grandma came out and told us to be quiet.'

And were you?

'For a minute, then we forgot. Grandma came out and said we were making so much noise that if we kept doing it, we'd kill the sparrow that was trying to get better. We'd frighten it to death.'

Were you quiet then?

'For a minute, then we forgot. Grandma came out again and sent Mick home, so I played on my own and when I went to feed it this morning it was dead.'

What did your mom say?

'She didn't say anything. She wrapped it in a bit of cloth from her sewing machine and put it in the bin when she thought I wasn't looking.'

What did Grandma say?

Remembering now full and well the waspish stupidity that had often slipped from those unthinking lips.

'I told you so.'

He turns away from me to study the milk-box on the wall, as if trying to see the bird still there, still resting, still outside of this bitter memory, then turns back.

'Do you still like me, mester?'

Always, and it wasn't your fault

'Is it alright though... to remember things like that... even when you're not sure?'

Yes. For a minute. And then forget

He hesitates a moment, and searches my face for I can't remember what, some kind of brand or secret sign of truth that only small boys know how to access.

Tell me some of your big ideas

'Well...' he says. He rotates his shoulders independently in a circular motion I'd quite forgotten, '...me and Mick are going to build a rocket ship.'

That's brave

'Mom says it's daft.'

What does your dad say?

'He says if I can make it work he'll give me the money to do it, but it won't cost much.'

Why?

He looks around the yard and at the bin I'm sat on,

'Me and Mick reckon that if we took four bins and fastened them all together on top of each other and put a pointed end on, it would be big enough, 'cept dad says it might take six if Wiggy's going, so we'll have to pinch some from the yard next door.'

So how does it work?

'In the Library there's a book and there's this rocket engine that looks like a cannon but it's firing all the time and if we put one of them in the bottom bin that should do it. Mick and me are saving up our fireworks this year to try it out. I copied the picture. I'm going to ask dad to get me some pipe from work.'

Sounds like a good idea to me

'Yeah, but it got me into trouble again.'

I laugh sympathetically, remembering the apprehension that fills this small but questing soul twisting his feet in the yard, knowing that he will always feel the weight of other eyes depressing his shoulder.

How did you manage that?

'I told my teacher. She caught me drawing it when I should have been listening. She told my mom.'

What did mom say?

'She wanted to know where I got it from, this talk about rocket ships and space. I said that things like thoughts didn't have to come from anywhere, not like people. You can make them up from bits of things. Like making up a rhyme. They're things you can have on your own and they're nobody else's. That's what I think.'

He shuffles up onto the bin next to mine, his eyes searching me sideways, devouring the small logo on my tee-shirt.

'Is that true, mester?'

Never more so than now, Billy

I know that will be too cryptic for him, but I also know that he will remember the particular shape of this verbal jigsaw piece.

He reaches a slow, tentative finger across the gap between us. I watch it crawl cross fifty years and a billion freed ergs of energy to point unerringly at the Jacquard logo on my breast.

He continues, absorbed by the stitching, almost detached from the words he is speaking.

'Teacher told Mom I shouldn't be thinking about things that can never happen. I should be doing my spelling instead. But that's too easy,' His face colours slightly, 'I can always do that. Teacher says nobody can ever go to space so why bother to think about it.'

What do you think?

He slowly retracts his hand and drops them both into his lap, head down in thought, trying hard to put the words together. At that moment, I want more than anything else in the world to just put my arms around him and hold on tightly. To let him know things that I dare not say. But I never can.

'I think… that if we don't think about things… then they can *never* happen. Will it ever happen, mester?'

What?

'Space… and things.'

If you think about them, much, much more than that will happen. What would you like to do most?

'Go to space,' he says without hesitation, then adds, cautiously, 'and drive a train.'

Which first?

'Dunno,' he says, shrugging off a decision, 'Either.'

He looks across the yard away from me and I know, even without seeing, that I would recognise the screwed lip and the squint that means he is thinking over something he's seen or heard that has attached itself to a deeper thought pattern, one that rarely surfaces beyond a silent barrier of improbability in his head.

'That badge,' he says, 'The one on your shirt. What is it?'

Four bins… with a pointed end on the top

He whirls around to stare at me in disappointment, the originality of his original, haunting vision of space already beginning to crumble behind his eyes.

'So you thought about it, too.'

I didn't need to. It was enough that you did. You and a lot of other people

The sun threads itself through a cloud and his eyes catch up the light again.

'You mean… I'm not daft on my own?'

Never. There are lots of us. The ones that think they aren't daft are the ones that don't think. Then when they're in trouble or need something, they come looking for us

'To tell us off?'

I choke down hard on the laugh that rises, an inevitable bubble of hope that we share so intimately. I smile in restraint.

Only after we've saved them

'Saved them from what?' his look of puzzlement almost complete.

Dragons in caves

'That's my *best* secret!' he says, 'How do you know about that? Did mom tell you?'

No. I just know. But how do you know?

He slides off the bin lid to land back on his feet, takes two short steps away into the sunlight then spins on his heel,

'I listened outside the teacher's door. She told mom that all I ever painted was pictures of dragons coming out of caves. She said I must be scared of something. She said there might be something wrong with me. With that and the rocket ship as well. Do you think there's something wrong with me, mester?'

Absolutely. There's something terribly, wonderfully wrong with you

He stares at me with totally expressionless eyes but I can see they are a mask that conceals all the troubles and unapportioned blame that the world will ever present.

'What's wrong with me, mester? Do I need a Doctor?'

No. The Doctor needs you

He shrugs, despondent, dissatisfied with my response.

'Dunno what *I* can do.'

You can think, can't you?

'What about?'

Anything you like, that's your real best secret

'Such as?'

I look away for the first time since I've arrived. I don't want him to see the potential dishonesty behind my eyes, the fear of discovery, the knowledge that even at seven he is capable of discerning why I am here, the gift I've come to steal... the gift of that sheer unalloyed spike of inspiration, unsullied by too many fears and funereal doubts, hiding within the fragmentary sharps and flats of his belief that all things can sing.

I don't want him to share in the uncertainty of my position, or allow him to see that at some time in the future, even *he* will run out of ideas.

Want to hear my secret?

'Yes,' he says.

Come closer

His feet shift without hesitation, then pull back, innate common sense dropping into play. More than aware of his sense of preservation, I reach into my pocket and draw out a sea shell, identical to the one in his own hand moments earlier.

I push it out of the shadow towards him, turning it slowly.

See the whorls in the shell? The way they are identical but getting smaller as we travel backwards in time to where the snail was born?

He takes out his and I place them carefully together on his upturned palm. Slowly, they meld into one. His face shines up at me, his eyes alight with answers already found, studied and discarded, chasing each other along the fever of his imagination. He snatches the shell and drops it in his pocket.

'How did you do that?'

I don't know. It shouldn't, but it always does it. Want to hear my secret?

He moves closer and I whisper into his ear the one Time Paradox I can't resolve.

He steps back suddenly, an exaggerated expression manifest across his face, infinitely recombining each left-over piece of aeroplane kit we have ever assembled without the instructions. He plunges his hands deep into both pockets, lost in thought for a moment, then draws out again the single shell. He holds it up to the sun so that the growth lines show dark against the pink light energy wavering through.

'What if... ?' he says.

I listen closely to him... and hear the clock he sets ticking in my head.

Origins

To be 'Specific', this story, perhaps little more than an elevated pun, although based on real historical figures and their reported attitudes and morality, attempts to demonstrate the difference between rigidly held beliefs and thoughts, and those whose minds are open and able to exploit that rigidity to the benefit of all. I have long acknowledged that we establish unnecessary patterns in our lives, religion being a major contributor to this, or have them established for us at an early age by a high degree of mis-parenting and poor quality education. This malpractice leaves society as trains, following the same direction but separated by an inability to change ideological tracks.

This creates a world where cross-fertilisation of ideas, concepts, and even races and individuals, becomes a minefield of rigid thinking, so much so that it is almost impossible to make the intellectual leap across to a place of greater safety and understanding.

Luckily, there are points along the line where change can become possible. These points are usually made by gifted individuals with a bravery of intellect that defies the set patterns that surround and stifle us.

Charles Darwin was one such.

Origins

October 2nd. 1836

'Hold ye that line!'

The shuffle of rope-soled espadrilles stopped abruptly at the bark of Fitzroy's voice. The gangplank rattled noisily against the gunwhale as the last of the men on it stepped lightly to the quay, becoming suddenly aware that the stones did not move under their feet.

On deck, the remainder of the line unshouldered their bags and laid them on the deck.

'Mr Wickham. That man there.'

The lieutenant took hold of a seaman by the shoulder.

'This one…?'

'Yes. His name, man.'

Wickham shook the shoulder held tightly in his grasp. The seaman stuttered a reply.

'Melville… Sir.'

'Hand me that bag.'

Melville picked up the bag and laid it gently at the Captain's feet. The bag settled, the canvas folds drifting slowly into the shapes of salt-stiffened clothes, native carvings and the idle moments of scrimshaw within. As the Captain watched, the folds shifted and rippled. Melville's face paled to the sheen of a scrubbed deck.

'Open it, man.'

FitzRoy stood over the bag, his expression filled with the surety of being twenty-eight years old and in total command.

Melville's hands shook as he bent to the bag. He fumbled at the buttons until FitzRoy swiped him out of the way with his stick.

'Mr Wickham. Let us bear witness to what he has here.'

Wickham bent tentatively to the bag, undid a button, then just as quickly drew away his hands as the bag rippled quietly again. He looked up at Melville who nodded. He undid the last two buttons and stood back. FitzRoy prodded Melville with the end of the stick.

'Take it out, man.'

'Sir…'

The stick lanced out again, this time catching Melville unawares in the rib. He grunted and scowled at the unjust pain.

FitzRoy was now in his element. Melville could sense his anger rising and reinforcing the one thing they had all learned during this voyage, that FitzRoy did not carry the nickname of 'Hot Coffee' for little reason.

'Enough man! Drag it out. Now. Or I shall have thyself and thy bag tipped unceremoniously over the side.'

Melville bent to open the flap of canvas, all the time expecting the cane to land smartly between his shoulderblades. He felt inside the bag until his fingers enclosed something soft and warm. He straightened and handed the dog to FitzRoy.

FitzRoy stepped back in amazement.

'What… what…?'

Wickham pulled it away from FitzRoy, horrified at what he saw. He dragged Melville around by the shirt.

'What meanest thou by this? Thou knowest the order…'

'Wait…' FitzRoy held his stick in the air.

Poised as it was between them, Melville knew that a twist of the handle would reveal a slender blade of shining steel, of which he had no desire to make the aquaintance.

FitzRoy lowered the stick until the end touched the animal.

'How *darest* thou…'

Melville cast his eyes to the deck. The sun bounded up from it with only half the power he had witnessed a few weeks before, adrift then in other latitudes where the sun was not the only thing that would willingly flay men's backs.

'Thou hast contravened a direct order. Thou art aware that, as Captain of a vessel afloat, I have the authority to hang thee?'

Wickham cast a glance to the for'ard capstan, where the rope bound it into creaking protest as the tide came in to take up the slack. FitzRoy followed his gaze and took the inference.

'Mr Wickham, shall I give the order to cast off again, make sail from port until we can find somewhere we can comfortably hang him?'

Wickham studied the faces of the men remaining in line behind Melville, and found it in him to respond.

'Sir. There is a time for example when there is a need for men to be so driven. Let us drive these men ashore with a lasting example of mercy under command. They may follow another more willingly.'

'And where, Wickham, in the annals of the Admiralty, does it state that willingness stands in the stead of duty?'

'I merely suggest, Sir, that duty may be enhanced by willingness. A willing ship may yet sail fairer seas.'

'Attend to thy scribbling, Wickham. Leave discipline to myself if thou finds it seemingly difficult to comprehend.'

Wickham's face flushed fiercely. He was acutely aware of the Captain's disregard for the journal he had written during the voyage. FitzRoy had found him at the chart table one evening, compiling by lamplight, the sperm oil bright and unsputtering. The Captain had snatched it from beneath his quill, read a few lines and thrown it to the floor in disgust.

'There are men on board who are paid to inscribe, Wickham. What pallid sense of journalism is thine? What lack of wit aboard thy quill?'

Melville tucked the dog beneath his arm where it shivered in the unaccustomed sunlight. The day was late, October-ish in the way that month performs solely for the English with their strained complexions and subtly-weighted clothes.

The dog remained silent, trained by Melville not to speak, although unaware of the reasons and the salvation that silence had bought throughout the remainder of the voyage.

The gangplank rattled once against the side of the ship and was stilled, but the silence surrounding the three men was impenetrable; eyes locked in a limited arc of awareness that existed peculiarly for them.

'Mr Wickham. Kill this damned abomination.'

'Sir…?'

'Now, man. Before we are all damned for eternity. Now, man!'

Wickham reached for the dog. The dog, sensing ill will, retreated further under Melville's arm and emitted a low growl. Wickham stood back in alarm.

FitzRoy exploded in anger.

'For the sake of Our Lord, man. Do as I say. Hast thou *no* spine?'

His steel blade inched out from inside the cane.

'Nay! I shall save the rope and run them through together...'

FitzRoy drew back his arm. The steel caught the sunlight in a bright flash that illuminated briefly the whole of Melville's life. He tucked the dog further against him, half-turning to shield it from the blade, although the wicked pervasiveness of that steel was well known.

FitzRoy found his hand clamped by that of another. The tip of the blade wavered in the air.

'Mr Darwin! How darest thou interfere with matters of ship's discipline!'

"Hold that blade, FitzRoy. How darest thou attempt the murder of one of my specimens? Along with that of an innocent seaman?'

FitzRoy allowed Darwin to lower the tip of the blade, then shook himself free of the grip and replaced the blade within the cane but, significantly, did not twist to lock the handle.

'Thou shalt not ever set foot on an Admiralty ship again.'

'FitzRoy, after five long years in thy company, I assure thee I have little desire to.'

FitzRoy twisted the lock on the cane handle.

'How do'st thou claim this ... animal... as thine own. Knowing well the origin of its progeniture?'

'I find it instrumental. As with many things, it is but a piece in the puzzle of the origin of all species. An unwitting but welcome adjunct to the completion and furtherance of my work. Mark thee well, FitzRoy...' he reached out to comfort the shaking animal. Melville turned it within reach of his gentle touch, '...that if thou would'st pin the word 'abomination' in the air between us, thou would'st be well to heed that Eve span from Adam's rib, and attach it just as firmly to thyself.'

FitzRoy tucked the cane under his arm.

'Have care, Mr Darwin. I fear thou hast fallen beneath Wickham's quill.'

Darwin reached for the dog under Melville's arm. The dog, sensing the easy release of pressure, exchanged hands willingly. Darwin hefted it against his shoulder.

'Thou see'st here, FitzRoy, an Eden on its day so thinly populated that Adam found only Eve. God gave *him* no choice in the matter, and he found himself as subtly subverted as thine own sire was by the bitch thou brought with him.'

'But... but...' FitzRoy stalled for words, 'But thine is the most specious of argument... and to bring the Bible into disrepute is worthy of a good hanging in itself. Mr Wickham? Is it too late to warp ship out into the river where I can end this blasphemy once and for all?'

'I'm afraid so, Sir. A coach has just drawn to the quay bearing Admiralty arms. I suspect that news of our arrival has already reached the City.'

'Then what *do* I have time for, Wickham?'

'A graceful retreat, Sir.'

'Wickham?'

'I have no other idea, sir.'

'Then scribe one, Wickham, when thou must. And I would have sight of it.'

FitzRoy retreated to his cabin. As he entered, his favourite dogs roamed and twisted playfully around his feet. He bent and stroked their ears. For once, his voice unusually soft as he spoke to them.

'How could'st thou this? Thou art brother against sister. What thinkest thou?'

The dogs licked at his hands, then shook out their long ears, hiding the slants of their eyes partially behind them as if contrite and reclusive, sharing a blame for something of which they knew naught.

A breeze took the window, slamming it out against the stern timbers. The air played around his hands, cooling them, changing his thoughts to the singularity of polar waters, the southern destitute latitudes where isolation knocked at the door of every man's thoughts.

He lifted the ears of Erin, sister to MacCoul.

'And how found thyself at the gates of this Eden? How solitary? I thought that thou would'st find companionship… in the way I might with mine own siblings. How base thy level then, to which I can never attain? And if I can never attain this, then how can I blame thee? On deck thou art blessed by progeny that I can never let thee see. Because if I let thee share in that, I can then only blame myself for the order that drowned his siblings. Thinking it rightful at that time, I can never apportion myself a share of that blame. So how can I salve thee? With words to which thou do'st not listen? With language, like that of Wickham, which is overly convulsed? Nay. I can only let him live… but far away from thee and thy scent.'

FitzRoy returned to the deck.

'Mr Darwin… I shall allow thee to remove this… this… from my sight. I shall not offend thee with explanation save to state that thou knowest his true origin.'

Darwin nodded a slight bow of gratitude, although he had never the intention of allowing the dog to remain on board, whatever the personal cost.

'I thank thee with grace, Captain. Be assured thou shall find favour in my journal.'

He turned to the seaman and handed back the dog.

'Melville. Take the dog down to the quay and await the arrival of myself on shore. Move not thyself nor let him loose.'

Melville felt his arm in the tight grip of Darwin and being led without hesitation across the quay, through an archway and into the inn yard beyond where, behind them, the prow of the ship was framed as if in cameo.

Melville found himself thrust down onto a rude bench beside a table. Darwin raised an arm and a girl came across to them.

'Decent beer. Two.'

The girl went away. Melville stroked the dog absently.

'I know not what to say to thee.'

'Then say little. Ignorant prattle has been my fare for the hour past. I care for none more. What will'st thou do with the animal?'

'I know not sir. I fear I cannot keep him. If I sail again, I shall not be able to take him on board.'

'Especially with FitzRoy, eh?'

Melville nodded. Darwin took hold of the beer as the girl laid it to the table.

'I have an idea, Melville. Art thou game?'

He caught hold of the girl's wrist.

'Art thou game, too, maid?'

'For what, Sir?' she replied, drawing back her wrist.

'For this…'

He took the young dog from Melville and handed it to her.

'It hath need of thy good services.'

'Oh, Sir. I am not sure.'

'Come now, maid. It will not trouble thee overmuch, being of a kindly disposition, as thyself may fairly be described.'

'I thank thee, sir. I do not deserve that, I am sure, but the dog does seem kindly disposed toward myself. By what name shall I call it?'

Darwin looked across the table at Melville expectantly.

'Well, man?'

Melville coloured slightly. He shuffled on the bench then spoke in a whisper.

Darwin nudged him.

'Speak up man. We can't hear you.'

'Dick, Sir… Moby Dick.'

'What sort of a name is that, man?'

'It's… more of a family tradition, Sir.'

'Ah, I see. And from where comes that tradition, as indeed thyself, sailor?'

'The Americas, Sir.'

'That explains much. I have heard there are many such peculiarities in that ungracious land.'

The dog nipped playfully at the girl's fingers.

'Would the Sirs mind if I chose my own name for him?'

Darwin waved his hand expansively.

'Feel free… eh, Melville?'

'It's just that, Sirs, if he misplaced himself, I would look a right fool going about calling his name.'

Darwin reached up to stroke the dog one last time.

'Call him a name as comely as thyself, maid.'

'I shall call him Rochester, Sir. I hope it finds thee with favour.'

'Just so, Miss…?'

'Eyre, Sir. Jane.'

'Just so. A comely enough appellation.'

'Thank thee kindly sir, but one more thing… if thy will grant…'

Darwin nodded his quiet aquiescence.

'What breed of dog is he, sir?'

Darwin turned to look back out of the courtyard, through the low archway to where the prow of the ship remained docked and visible, his home, willing or not, for good or ill, for the last five years, and realised how much and how little he would miss her.

He turned back and smiled.

'A Beagle, madam… A Beagle.'

Cheval

Mirrors fascinate me. Every time I go to see a new optician I have a question that I ask. So far, I have a different answer from each optician. And I don't believe any of them. The question, simply put, is this. What do we really see in a mirror? The pragmatic answer is that we see light reflected from a surface just below the glass and that we see ourselves reversed, our 'mirror image', and that this image exists solely on that silvered surface.

Don't believe it. Try this little experiment.

If, like myself, you need glasses for reading, then you will know what focal length has been set for you. Usually around two feet or so, the comfortable place to hold a book. Now stand two feet away from a mirror and hold the book beside your head and you can't read it, although the image is the required two feet away. (yes, I know it's in reverse.) Now move in until you *can* read it. You'll find yourself one foot away. But wait a minute... if that image exists only on the silvering behind the glass and is two feet away, you should see it perfectly. But you don't. You have to move in to half the focal length. So where is the image? Does it actually exist at all? Please write in with your own theory...

Einstein's Theory of Relativity states that the experience of Time is relative to the velocity of the observer and that objects travelling at different speeds experience time at different rates.

As humans we are relatively slow creatures who observe time slipping by at speeds we can never hope to achieve.

But what if we are not the slowest things in the Universe, what if the things that seem static around us are travelling too, but so slowly that we can't see the change? Even in a mirror...

To Janna this was just a game she played as a child, but it was a game she believed in all her life... right up to the end.

Cheval

The trick was not to let them see you.

Janna had played this game before and knew that there was this one cardinal rule. *They mustn't see you!* She lay flat, as close as she could to the floorboards. She knew no-one would mind the dust on her dungarees as long as she was up here in the half-dusk of the loft amongst the old discoveries that always seemed new and fresh to her, instead of being downstairs and underfoot.

Stay low! Move slowly!

Janna edged across the room, her nose following the line of a joint in the boards directly over to where the bound chest squatted like a fat old frog in a dark forgotten corner with its mouth set in a straight line and an unmistakable smugness about its whole expression. She pulled herself into its shadow and rested. She peeked over the tired, curved leather of the lid.

They hadn't seen her!

Their wooden stallion eyes looked straight out across the room as if they could see right through the roof and the tiles and the nails and all the years of dust into somewhere she couldn't see, perhaps another place they were charging to even now as she hid behind the chest watching them, waiting to see them move, aching, wanting them to be free and to run high-stepping across all the dusty boards and out into the sunlight where they could flash and snort and buck and run and just… be.

Janna wondered if maybe they moved all the time. It didn't seem right to have all that power and energy frozen into shapes that didn't move and only ever threatened to burst into life. She felt as if they had always known what it was like to run, but for now they were only resting and watching.

Some days she wondered if maybe they moved too slowly for her to see, like a petal opening, or a flower closing, or the sun in the sky at midday when the birds swoop and swirl around, teasing it on towards evening, and just maybe if she closed her eyes and only opened them now and again she might be able to see that they had moved …like when you mark the sun with a stick in the ground the way that her grandpa had shown her and said that was how you knew and that it didn't do to keep looking at things the whole time 'cause you never saw the changes and as how that went for people too.

She had thought of marking the boards where their hooves pushed against them with a piece of chalk, but they would see her and just sit and wait until she had rubbed it out again or the dust had covered it and they could move again in their own quiet time, despite the way their nostrils flared and their eyes stared open and wild into space and their hooves flailed the air, threatening the dust motes.

Janna had always wondered where it was that they were looking, what it was they were seeing that she couldn't, and why.

She came out from behind the chest and lay on the floor in front of them, her chin on the backs of her folded hands. She closed her eyes and counted... one... two... three...

Inside her head she could hear the growing stomp of hooves galloping, galloping, closer and closer until it seemed she would be struck into the dust and the boards beneath her hands began to shake with the pressure of horses and wildness and freedom and she felt that the whole loft was about to open like the petals of a flower while she wasn't looking and that they would burst upwards and outwards and that she would be with them, clinging to the scent of manes and flying tails and they would move across the sky calling out to the sun as they passed until they reached the top of a large hill where they could rest and the horses could bend their necks and shake their heads into tall cool grass and perhaps just once, if she was very patient, she might see that their eyes had closed and the deep strong breath they had held tight in their jutting chests all those years had been let out and that they were satisfied and full and free.

Janna opened her eyes.

They were still there.

They were still there because between them they formed the feet and carried the dark base of a tall, slender, oblong mirror wrapped tightly in several layers of white sheet and taped firmly around the corners ...as if whoever had wrapped it had expected a wind to blow through the loft ...scattering sheets and dusts and toppling picture frames and memories ...covering them in the shifting sands of what may or may not be fashionable anymore.

Some time later Janna climbed back up the loft ladder. Only this time she had no choice but to let them see her. She sat on the floor beside them with her swollen, fertile belly and gently blew the dust from their nostrils, blew the layers from their eyes, blew like the long-expected wind over their manes and tails and dared to stroke the undersides of their hooves despite their frozen imminence.

She was now no longer half-afraid of them. Their dark wood carving shone in the light from the pale yellow of the bulb but now, somehow, the magic was gone. She closed her eyes and opened them again. They were still there, only this time she didn't expect them to move, didn't expect them to soar over and above her in one stride to freedom, didn't expect them to be looking at other lands, couldn't find the hill top or feel tall cool grass between her toes.

She knew, also, that she would let out her last breath before they did, and that if they did move, which, despite all she had ever come to know she still believed that they did, it was with the speed of light crossing the universe, so slow and ponderous beside the world outside that their journey would last forever and that what she had seen was just a blink in their passing, a split-second still-frame freeze out of eternity, and no-one could close their eyes for that long, except that one day she would, and perhaps if she waited long enough, she would open them again onto a bright sky filled with darkly carved wooden horses bucking and running, with small girls clinging to manes and tails and calling out and birds teasing passing suns. She smiled and began to lift the edges of the tape that held the sheets in place above them.

As she took off the last piece of tape the sheets fell away. Beneath them was a mirror, its silvering kept perfect against the years by the careful way in which it had been swaddled against time, the only wind ever to blow through the loft.

As the sheet fell away Janna thought that for an instant she might have caught a flicker that wasn't her own reflection, wasn't the pale yellow of the same old bulb, then dismissed it as the dust settled around her, coating the horses once more, blinding their eyes again.

She looked at herself in the glass. She was less than tall but it took only a second to see that she had confidence. It was in the way she stood and the way she smiled back at herself and the way her eyes fell short of forever as if they were now fastened to the earth and for once seeing things that were and things that mattered and things that had to be done and not wished for and how, somehow, the magic had gone a little from her too. She dropped the sheet back over the mirror.

She would give it away ...tomorrow.

Some time later, Janna climbed back up the loft ladder and eased herself onto the floor. She paused a moment to catch her breath and look at her palms that were covered in dust. She smacked them together and climbed to her feet. She shuffled the four steps across to the mirror and pulled off the sheet that loosely draped over it. In the instant before the light from the pale yellow bulb cracked back at her from the glass, she saw something that moved so fast that for a moment she was almost convinced she had seen herself all that time ago, when movement was grace and ease and taken for granted.

She smiled. Had she ever really had that magic? She patted the grey of her hair and looked for the reflection that would show her as she was, when she too had lines and angles and curves that moved too fast for the dust to settle on, but it was buried too far down, too deep into the glass for her to stand here and try to pull it out when there may not be enough time for things that only move at the speed of light, and how you should savour all that you have and not wish for more or for things that are gone.

She shook the sheet over the mirror. As it settled down against the glass, she thought she saw... she thought she saw

...no. Just the bulb. Just these old eyes up to tricks a body could never dream of or explain if they had forever. The thought seemed to stick in her mind, rattling like a tramcar past shop windows and shimmering the reflections with the whine and the chatter of its wheels until they settle down again and suddenly everything becomes crystal clear like a pond when the ripples have died and the fish glide like thoughts into the mouths of streams they knew were there but had forgotten, it seems, only yesterday.

She went downstairs to wait and to think and to climb back down that long passing ladder of light into the dust and dark corners under the sheets and tapes in her head.

Some time later Janna climbed back up the loft ladder and paused at the top.

The trick is not to let them see you.

Janna had played this game before and knew that there was this one cardinal rule.

They mustn't see you!

She lay flat, as close as she could to the floorboards. She knew there was no-one left to mind about the dust on the summer print of her housecoat, or that she was up here in the half-dusk of the loft.

The house was empty and she thought that for a while it might not mind her not being there when it called out with a leaking tap or a creaking board or a shelf that had borne up so well until at last it too had gone the way of all things.

She looked at the stuff around her, and the old bound chest. She had forgotten what was in there and perhaps if it wasn't worth remembering, then perhaps it wasn't worth the effort and it would sit there forever smiling its thin-lipped smile and never get to croak.

She felt, like the house, that she was at the end of a long book, with most of it opened and the rest feeling kind of thin under her thumb and some of the corners creased and uncomfortable in ways that she didn't care to think about any more.

Stay low! Move slowly!

With her nose to the line of a joint in the floorboards, Janna dragged herself across into the shadow of the old chest and peeked over the tired, curved leather of the lid.

They hadn't seen her!

She reached around and caught the corner of the sheet that was draped across the mirror and slowly pulled it to the floor. From the glass shone a pale yellow light, and beneath it Janna could see the green of tall, cool grass, and in the grass, bending their necks and shaking their heads, were two horses, dark as dusty corners and powerful as hidden smiles, with flared nostrils ...and wild, wide eyes that could see forever.

A Small Commotion

…was written specifically in another attempt to access the shortlist of the (Irish) Fish Prize. I'd had a story included in the anthology of prize-winners in 2001, a story included earlier in this book as 'To Kill a Wish', and convinced myself that, if it had an Irish feel to it and was set in Dublin, I might just sneak it in there. No chance. I got the long list. Never mind.

Here's another story…

'A Small Commotion' was written at a time when I was dabbling with pencil drawing. I say dabbling because that's what it was and not much more, even though it was very enjoyable. I'm not bad at it but it doesn't 'flow' like it should. (I'm too anal about detail, as you might have noticed if you've read this far.) You should know what's coming next… you see, my birthday is Christmas Day so it makes it doubly difficult for people to find original presents for me, and… one hint of a hobby and you are showered with tranklements for it.

I am now the proud owner of enough high quality pencils to last the lifetimes of myself and my twin grandchildren who appeared on the 26th. November 2016, Bless 'em.

A Small Commotion

Gilly walked into the bar late of one September evening. Outside, O'Connell Street shone wet beneath a sky that was no more than a momentary blossom of promise while tomorrow's rain lay still dark of the horizon, drowning a sun like the burn in Gilly's throat. Once inside, he hung his derby on the rack beside the door and ordered a pint of stout.

Taking a great draught of ale, he pulled in the blue haze, well-rubbed atmosphere of the early bar, mostly filled by people with movement in the way they set, trying not to get too comfortable in case the night and the drink took them unawares. Gilly took the gill that remained in his glass and moved across to his usual table, setting it down dark against the polished copper.

Beside him a small commotion was raised, with laughter curling the smoke above the table in the corner. There was Timulty, dark, fiery eyed, bellowing great guffaws beside Mulrooney's broken, leprous grin, and across from them O'Keefe, the quiet, the listening. In their midst was a great man whose skin shone with the glow of a pale autumn and whose eyes pushed them back into their seats from where his words teased the laughter out of their wet-day, rain-tomorrow faces.

Gilly hadn't seen him before, he would have remembered that great shock of sun-bleached hair.

He slid farther along the bench to listen until Timulty saw him, 'Gilly! Gilly, come here!'

Gilly blushed, as though he'd been caught eavesdropping.

'Come here and meet Clancy. Just this minute from over the water.'

Gilly slid up towards them as Timulty turned to the great man, 'Clancy. This is Gilly. Gilly from the Bank.'

The man's hand moved towards him. Gilly viewed it with some apprehension until Clancy gave a short barking laugh.

'Come on, now,' he said, 'Don't be afraid to shake the steadiest hand this side of the water.'

He turned it slowly in the mid-air, 'Look! Five pints and not a tremor!'

He turned his head away to see the smiles on the other faces, 'A wager on the sixth?'

Gilly studied the dregs of his glass. 'I'll get them,' he said.

He returned from the bar to find a space had been made for him beside Clancy. As he sat, the conversation fell around the table towards him.

'Over the water?' he said.

'Aye,' said Clancy, 'The Pond. The Big One.'

'American?' asked Gilly, marvelling at the stupidity of his own question.

'Aye. Second generation.'

Mulrooney sniggered. Clancy pulled darkly at the new pint of stout, 'My Granfer. Pushed out by the blight in '45. Settled in Chicago and promised himself he would grow nothing anymore except older.'

'What happened to him?' asked Gilly.

Clancy's smile wrinkled the corners of his eyes, 'Why, he died. Same as the fuckin' rest of us!'.

Mulrooney giggled at Gilly's discomfort. Timulty's eyes fell dark and O'Keefe sat watching, as if he were waiting for a sudden, more sullen cue to laughter.

'But before he did,' said Clancy, '...he planted the seed of old Ireland into my father and now here I am come back like a ghost to see what it is you've got, and to tell you what it is you're missin'.'

'And for sure we don't have much.' said Mulrooney.

Clancy laughed out loud, 'God, man. This country! It's beautiful! Don't you ever look up when it stops raining?'

'Ah, we would,' said Timulty, '...if it ever stopped fuckin' rainin'.'

'Ah! You don't know what a jewel you have,' said Clancy, 'Why, I've been to places where they haven't seen water for years.'

'Then what do the landlords put in the beer?' asked Timulty.

'Is America... a desert, then?' said Gilly.

Mulrooney sniggered once more, but Clancy turned to Gilly beside him, 'Only of the soul, my friend. But compared with what I saw from the train on the way up from Dublin, the whole world is a desert. I tell you, you don't know what you have. This place is a jewel and a treasure.'

'Gilly knows all about treasures,' said Mulrooney.

'I forgot,' said Clancy, his eyes fixed to Gilly's, 'you're from the Bank.'

'Oh no,' said Mulrooney, 'He has one of his own. Keeps it locked up these days. We don't see much of it anymore. A real Jewel!'

'Excuse me,' said Clancy, reading the look of quiet embarrassment on Gilly's face, 'But this has the sound of a woman about it.'

'Ah!' said O'Keefe, '…and what a woman.'

'I remember the times,' said Timulty, '…when he used to parade her around the town like a peacock.'

'Aye,' said O'Keefe, laughing, '…then he'd drop her at the corner of Saint Steven's so she could walk the last fifty yards by herself because her father was a big man and didn't like the look of poor old Gilly!'

'And we'd follow 'em around,' said Mulrooney, '…discreetly o'course, and watch her sway down the street with our mouths open an' lumps in our trousers an' our tongues draggin' all over the pavement.'

'Sounds like some woman!' said Clancy.

'Some,' said Timulty.

'Some an' a half,' said Mulrooney with a leer, 'We'd take a line behind 'em until they got to the corner o' Merrion, then we'd sideswipe by Ely St. into Hume in a huge clatter of our ould boots where Gilly couldn't hear us, just in time to see her arse swashing up the steps to the house.

'Sometimes you make me sick,' said Gilly, rising from his seat.

'Now, now,' said Clancy, suddenly becoming a hand on his shoulder, a whisper in the ear, 'Don't take on so. The boys didn't mean any harm. They're just jealous, and of what I might never know. Seeing as you keep her locked up.'

'I do not,' said Gilly, 'It's just that, it's not long since the weddin' and, well, since the Hospital, she doesn't seem to want to go out so much.'

'Oh, I'm sorry to hear that,' said Clancy, 'I hope she's feelin' better soon.'

Gilly slid his face behind an upturned glass.

'Nah!' said Mulrooney, 'It wasn'a her. It was him!'

He leaned the long meanness of his face up to the table.

'Kicked square in the nuts by a dray horse. Right out there in the back yard on his way for a pee. There was blood and piss everywhere! He's now what you might call, a 'broken' man.'

Timulty flashed him a look that sat him back into his seat, his face outside the circle of light from the smoking, suspended lamp, where the broken spirit of his fingers could still be seen manipulating the air into huge shapes.

'Like the winnin' table at the Church vegetable show, he was. Except it was all the colour o' chopped liver.'

Timulty backhanded him in the ribs, 'Ya did'na see it.'

'Sister's a cleaner at the hospital. She told Ma.'

Mulrooney leaned forward once more into the light, the brown, broken teeth at once lascivious and obscene.

'Wurd is, his missus asked the doc if he could cure the pain and leave the swellin'.'

Gilly stood up to leave as Clancy's hand fell on his arm. Gilly shook his head, his face hidden in the shade.

'A man can make his mark in many ways,' said Clancy, '…be sure and remember that now.'

Gilly's face held like stone until he met the cool, moist air of O'Connell Street.

The following Sunday there was a knock at Gilly's door. He opened it to find Clancy pressed beneath the small porch away from the gentle rain. His collar was up but he had a look of open spaces about him, as though he were something wilder that had been caught and brought here to stand on a cold Irish doorstep one Sunday morning just to show Gilly how small the world really was.

'Come in,' said Gilly, holding open the door. Clancy brushed past him to stand in the hall.

'Go through into the parlour. Here, give me your coat. That's if you're for stayin'.'

'I think that depends on you,' said Clancy. Beneath the coat he wore a dark roll-neck jumper over dark trousers and fine black shoes. In his hand was a small leather case. He put this on the table and sat down.

'That's alright with me,' said Gilly, 'Even a broken man needs visitors.'

'Now, now!' said Clancy, 'That wasn't me.'

'I know,' said Gilly, 'They were just showin' off, is all.'

Clancy looked at his watch, 'You're not up to the Church then?'

Gilly sat down in the chair beside the fire, his eyes adrift with the flames,

'I kind of... lost the Faith a little. Or maybe I lost it altogether. I don't know. Perhaps only time will tell.'

The fire flecked his eyes with another kind of motion.

'You know,' he said, '...when a man has had the Faith all his life, it's hard to know what to hang on to when it's gone.'

Clancy knotted his long fingers on the table before him, said one word, 'Himself.'

'And what,' said Gilly, '...when a part of himself might be gone too. A vital part. A part that marks him as a man.'

'That's when,' said Clancy, '...he must find another way. Another way to make his mark.'

He opened the small leather case, laid back the lid across the embroidered linen of the cloth.

'Here is just one way. But this is my way and I'm not saying that it should be yours. This is just the way that I found.'

He took from the case a slender pencil in blue painted wood and laid it lovingly against the cloth.

'2B' he said, '...for the subtle Irish light.'

He took out another,

'HB... for the lines that only life can etch so deep.'

Gilly came to join him at the table, his mind tumbling back down to schooldays and the pure, inimitable power of a new pencil.

Clancy took out another, then another, laid them out in ranks beside the case. He reached into the bottom and produced a pad of fine vellum paper with the flyleaf folded back as if it were ready like a camera primed and plated to capture the fleeting moment. He closed the case and placed it beside him on the floor.

'I'm here,' he said, '...to collect your treasure.'

Gilly stepped back, 'Then you're no better than the rest of them,' he said, 'But at least you're honest.'

'No,' said Clancy, 'I'm here to take her for a moment, that's all, then give her back to you forever. Theirs is a greed. This is my gift to you.'

'Ah!,' said Gilly, 'I see! A gift for the broken man. Well I have no need of your pity. I'm surrounded by it as it is.'

Clancy smiled, 'You don't understand, but then that's my fault. Let me tell you. Some years ago, I found I had the ability to freeze time.'

'And for sure,' said Gilly, '...isn't life long and hard enough without a feller like you goin' around makin' it last forever?'

Clancy laughed out loud, 'I wouldn't if I could.'

'I'm awful pleased to hear it,' said Gilly.

'I'm talking about the moments,' said Clancy, 'like… have you ever looked out of a train window at speed and seen the sun bridge a lough like the warriors way to Valhalla and thought how much richer life would be if you could carry that feeling with you the whole way through, so that you could bring it out on dark days and remember that it isn't always so?'

He caressed the rigid pencils, 'I wouldn't take the speed out of life,' he said, 'That's what makes it vital and exciting. But every so often it should be marked, like a Plimsoll line, so that a man can see the load he's carrying and choose what to put down. You have a weight about you, Gilly. I'm here to make a mark on your life. Now, where's this treasure?'

'Up to the Church,' said Gilly.

'Then tea would be nice,' said Clancy, '…while we wait.'

Rebecca shook her way into the hall, the brolly rustling and rattling against the stand. She fingered the pale, unfamiliar, belted raincoat hung there and made through into the parlour, shedding her cape to leave it drying by the fire.

Gilly rose to his feet, 'Hello, my dove,' he said, 'I'd like you to meet Clancy.'

Clancy put down the cup before he dropped it. Gilly watched his face with a quiet smile, then, 'Clancy, this is my wife, Rebecca.'

Clancy took her hand gently as if it were a butterfly wing. He turned to Gilly,

'The Bridge to Valhalla!' he said.

'Is that near Dun Laoghaire?' said Rebecca.

'If you were there,' said Clancy, '…then that's where it's like to be.'

Rebecca took the gist of Clancy's words and flushed to the bone, 'Mr Clancy. I take you for an awful flatterer!'

'Please, it's just 'Clancy''

'Then it's just 'Rebecca',' she said.

She seated herself by the hearth and Clancy felt rubbed by the raw edge of her beauty. He watched her eyes smile across at Gilly who had sat down opposite so that he could draw off her boots to leave her toes warming by the fire, and this was no smile of condescension. This was a smile of pride and of purpose, a smile for a whole man.

Clancy studied her face as only an artist would. He admired the full height of cheekbone, the delicate drape of jawline curving away into long slender neck muscles held under tension by the tilt of her head as she in turn studied the look on Gilly's face as only a woman would.

Clancy began to feel that his presence was intrusive.

'I…' he said, then became aware that he had broken the spell. They turned to look at him from their places by the fire.

'Mr Clancy,' said Rebecca, 'I'm sorry. Sometimes we shut out the world, Gilly and I. There was no slight intended. It's just that…'

'It's alright,' said Clancy, picking up and studying the pencils, 'It's just that, having met you, I realise how ineffectual all of this seems.'

'Why, Mr Clancy,' said Rebecca, 'What do you have there?'

'Just pencils.'

'Pencils were never just pencils, Mr Clancy.'

'Right here, right now,' said Clancy, tumbling them from his fingers, '…that's how they feel.'

Rebecca came across to the table, 'No, no. Let me show you.'

She took a pencil from Clancy's hand, 'Look, now. My father always said that when they made a pencil, they made it from a piece of wood that had grown for years and seen all kinds of changes, and then they took it and made a hole right along the middle and into that hole they pushed all the pictures it would ever draw, just waiting for a child or an artist,' she looked deep into his eyes, '...although I think they might be one and the same, to come along and let them out.'

Clancy threw back his head with laughter.

'Oh, my dear Rebecca. You are both a treasure and a jewel, and a very perceptive eye.'

He watched Gilly who sat rocking by the fireside.

'And a veritable Plimsoll Line.'

He picked up the case and threw the pencils and the tablet inside as if suddenly they had lost all their worth.

'These will not do!' he said to Gilly, 'The Bridge to Valhalla should be gold, not the pathetic pewter of pencils. I find myself ashamed of the thought.'

Gilly smiled quietly and kept on rocking.

Rebecca straightened the cloth, 'Clancy,' she said, looking at Gilly, '...it would be our honour...'

Gilly nodded almost imperceptibly.

'...if you would stay for lunch. It isn't much split three ways, but it should suffice.'

'I'm sure it will be Ambrosia,' said Clancy, 'And I don't mind if I do.'

Gilly swayed, smiling, in the chair, pictures freezing in his minds eye like a great cataract of times and places and, caught in each one, was Rebecca.

The next day, Gilly met Clancy outside the Bank at lunch. Clancy filled him with a great excitement as they took O'Connell Street and into the bar.

'Gilly, she's a wonder! Now don't misunderstand me... And you have the money? Great! I'm sorry, I have my fare and board and lodgings but very little else.'

Gilly patted his coat pocket and ordered two stouts with ham and pickles to follow, along with a fair wedge of Stilton.

'I have the money,' he said, 'But you mustn't tell Rebecca. She'll only think me a fool.'

'Oh no,' said Clancy, 'She'll think you a great and a wise man. What better way to meet the future than to engrave a piece of your past and bring it right along with you. Without a reminder it would always seem like now, and nothing would seem to pass at all, and what kind of a future would that be if you didn't even notice you had one?'

Gilly smiled and handed over a five punt note.

'Great!' said Clancy, 'That will buy the easel and the brushes.'

Gilly coughed and handed over another.

'The canvas and the paint,' said Clancy.

'Remember,' said Gilly, 'No-one must know.'

Clancy raised his glass, 'To Valhalla!' he said.

'Just… where is that?' asked Gilly.

Clancy carried all the materials into Gilly's house the next Sunday when all were up at the Church and the street was quiet and the curtains had given up their twitching until after Mass. He unwrapped the brown paper and, with Gilly's help, set up the easel beside the south facing window of what Gilly called his 'study'. The walls were panelled in dark brown Lincrusta, scumbled to rosewood to match the shelves that carried Gilly's few books. The curtains were drawn back and the sun lit the lace with gold.

Rebecca caught them as they were unwrapping the paints.

'Don't tell me, Mr Clancy, I'm to have a portrait of Gilly?'

'It would be a fine portrait I'm sure, Rebecca.' He nodded at Gilly, '…but he's no Bridge to Valhalla.'

'Then what am I to have?'

'The pleasure of sitting for two weeks so that Gilly can have the look of you forever,' said Clancy.

'He already has me forever,' said Rebecca.

'Ah!' said Clancy, 'You know that and I know that. But Gilly?... well...'

Gilly flushed, 'I just want to have your youth and beauty to look at forever,' he said.

"tis a strange coincidence,' said Rebecca, '...for that's why I married you.'

Clancy sat Rebecca across from the window where he could have an eye on both her and the canvas.

'No, I don't like it,' he said, 'When the sun's as low as this the light's too harsh, the shadows too hard and sharp.'

'But it's a nice room,' said Rebecca, 'I feel at ease here, like I'm in control of something of Gilly's. It makes me want to smile.'

She pulled the pins from the clasp she wore, shook out the long flame of her hair into the sunlight where it caught and held,

'Don't you want to catch me when I'm happy?'

Clancy felt the breath stolen from him.

'Sure,' he said, then paused for thought, '...but it's not an Irish light. An Irish light is softened with the edges pushed around the corners giving everything a certain depth. This is more of an... English light.'

'That does it,' said Rebecca, 'The parlour it is.'

For two weeks Clancy watched the fire from the parlour range play within the blue of her eyes until he saw his own hand with jealousy, as though it were a stranger's, caressing her face with brush strokes. In all that time Rebecca never asked to see the painting, for which small mercy, Clancy was glad. Gilly himself watched it grow from the canvas as Clancy took the glow from the hearth and pushed it under her skin so that she seemed lit from within. At the end of the two weeks

Gilly had all he could ever have wished for. The painting was like a mirror.

'No,' said Gilly, holding it into the light, '...better than a mirror, for a mirror is hard and cold to the touch. This, is a reflection of her soul.'

'Clancy,' said Rebecca, 'You carry the guilt of making me more beautiful than I could ever be. How can I hope to live up to it?'

Clancy looked down at his hands, caught at the edge of the table to stop them shaking.

'In the two weeks I have been here,' he said, '...you have surpassed it times over.'

'Mr Clancy...'smiled Rebecca, 'I take you for an...'

'No,' said Clancy, 'Please don't give it the lie.'

He stared down at his hands, 'It's time I moved on.'

Gilly and Clancy parted at the bar. Clancy had been reluctant to meet there, he didn't want to see the look of expectation on the faces of Mulrooney and the others, nor could he ever have explained that to Gilly. He felt as though he were one of the lost boys, leaving behind something so precious he didn't dare try to remember what it was. Gilly paid him the thirty punt with much coughing but no denial.

When Gilly returned from the toilet, Clancy was gone, easel, brushes, paints and all, but standing inside the empty half-pint glass was a slender pencil in blue-painted wood. Gilly fitted his hand to the warmth of the glass as might have Clancy's a moment ago. He looked closely at the pencil.

'2B,' he said, '...for the subtle... Irish... light.'

Rebecca insisted that the painting hung in the parlour, right over the mantle.

'I pass it a hundred times a day,' she said, '…and it helps me remember how to smile when you're late home from the bar and inside I'm seething and sizzling like your dinner on the range.'

Gilly put his feet up on the fender and smiled.

Slowly the word got around the bar. There had been a man visiting Rebecca while Gilly himself was up at the Bank. Mulrooney had already caught the whisper. By description he knew who the visitor must be.

'Have you seen Clancy of late, Gilly?' he said.

'No,' said Gilly, '…and should I have?'

'Oh, no, no,' said Mulrooney, 'No reason. Though word has it you were in here with him last Monday evenin', and we haven't seen him since.'

He pulled his long strained look of a face up to Gilly's

'Wurd has it, that you was givin' him munny.'

'I'm always willin' to help a man down on his luck,' said Gilly, '…even on Bank wages.'

'Thirty Punt's a lot of luck to be down on,' said Mulrooney.

Timulty caught Mulrooney's arm, 'Leave him alone a minute. Can't you see the man is troubled.'

'Have you won the Sweepstake, Gilly?' he asked.

'No,' said Gilly, 'Not that it's anyone's business if I had.'

O'Keefe came round beside him and sat down.

'Now, now, Gilly. We're worried about you, is all. That's an awful lot of money to be givin' a man, no matter how far down he is.'

'Proppin' him up,' said Timulty. He shook his head, 'A fine gesture, and one becoming of you, but…'

'Buyin' him off!' shouted Mulrooney, 'Buyin' him off! We all know who he was visitin' while you was up at the Bank!'

Gilly hit him, with all the remembered force of a dray pony's hoof.

That evening Gilly took down the painting from over the mantle and hung it in the study out of sight. Next morning, after he was up to the Bank, Rebecca hung it back in the parlour. Gilly came home and took it down again and wouldn't say why. In the mornings, after Gilly was up to the Bank, she hung it over the mantle once more, always remembering to take it down before he came home.

He arrived home one night a little later than usual, and more than a little unsteady.

'Gilly, my love. Are you alright?' said Rebecca.

He settled down into the chair by the fire.

'I had to see O'Neill this afternoon.'

'The District man?' said Rebecca.

'Aye. The District man,' said Gilly, 'Seems he heard about the commotion at the bar last month.'

'What ruckus was that?'

'Oh,' said Gilly, 'Mulrooney was bein' himself as usual. Nothin' important.'

'Important enough for the District man to hear.'

'If it happens again I'm to be considered for the notice,' said Gilly.

'What should we do then, my love?'

Gilly closed his eyes and let the flames from the hearth flicker across their lids, flashing the insides with bright desert colours,

'There's always America,' he said.

'But Gilly, I don't want to live in America. I want to live here where it rains and where people look at you in the street and see you as you were when they themselves were young, and where the world is so small that we ourselves seem that much bigger by it.'

Gilly opened his eyes and she watched the desert fires die within them to be replaced by a softer, more subtle kind of light.

'It's alright,' he said, 'I have the measure of it. It was just a small commotion, and Mulrooney has spoken his last word upon the matter.'

Gilly closed his eyes again and watched his future sail on beneath a golden, glowing bridge into the arms of a natural harbour where the sea was flat and calm and filled with the light of many bright, untroubled suns.

'Then while you're feeling so fine and positive, will you please hang my painting back over the mantle?' said Rebecca.

'Of course I will, my love.'

Gilly smiled as she took to her knees to stare into the fire.

'As soon as my supper has settled.'

He put out his hand and touched the warm shock of her hair.

'Well,' said Rebecca, pulling the shoes from him as he rocked back in the chair, '... 'tis a fine time to be talking about losing your job. What with you still recovering your wits from the accident and your limp only now beginning to settle.'

She smiled up at him as only a woman would, '...an' me with child an' all.'

Obtuse

Being 'Obtuse', is of course, just another angle on life. Practised well, it becomes a cussed streak against any form of order or conformity until it acquires almost the status of a religion. Its practitioners, and I know many, find in it a source of wild expression that irritates the hell out of the rest of us.

This is a story of someone who has decided to place freedom of expression above all else. However, if you try to live like this, there is a cumulative effect that slowly builds into the catastrophic.

Some people wring change from every situation. Others wait patiently to have change wrought upon them.

Arthur was one such in his dour suit and undertakers shoes... until he met the redoubtable Mrs Eammon McCandless (Deceased), a great believer in the 'Obtuse'.

Obtuse

'Arthur,' said Mrs Eammon McCandless (Deceased), 'It seems that at this point in my life, I have discovered a passion for the ...*obtuse.*'

She toyed her large, fat fingers around a sea-jade tulip vase from the mantel.

Arthur looked down at his black undertakers shoes, his pipe-stem ankles, and the way his little toes bulged the leather like a whole dam of spent miles about to burst, and remained silent.

'McCandless himself,' the widow went on, '...was a great believer in *perfection.*'

Arthur turned his gaze to the fly with the damaged wing orbiting the lightshade.

'But one can certainly tire of that,' she added, with an air of finality.

She took the urn that Arthur had brought and tipped the remains of Eammon McCandless (Deceased) into a huge pink onyx ashtray, and smiled a great, deep, secret smile. She stared intently at Arthur who sat there with hair awry and the sleeves of his coat hung limply from slender, indifferent and uneven shoulders.

'But you,' said Mrs McCandless, 'Arthur... you have *possibilities.*'

For six months, Arthur and Mrs Eammon McCandless shared a bliss that, given her new-found reluctance to submit to any form of perfection, was without doubt a veritable feast of discord and asymmetry. After the first month a leg fell from the bed as they lay there laughing in irregularity and disarray at their own good fortune. Arthur moved to fix it.

'*Obtuse,*' roared Mrs McCandless, 'It's quite obvious that it was no longer able to cope with such order as to be one corner of a square! Let it be! Let it be... *obtuse!*'

In time, Arthur came to find that obtuseness hard to bear, with the bed having collapsed upon his only pair of shoes and now he was left with just the new, single left shoe Mrs McCandless had brought him from the rummage sale. The other, said Mrs McCandless '...was probably off somewhere being... *obtuse.*'

Within a few months more, the house was a wreck. Mostly it went unnoticed as Arthur and Mrs McCandless veered from outright displacement to dissimilarity with great glee in each others capacity for discordance, until nothing was left that didn't either lean or fall when touched, or wouldn't close, or was jammed shut, or juxtaposed in nauseating unfamiliarity with the least of its neighbours.

By the end of December, the house was freezing. The windows wouldn't close and the doors were either missing or ajar. Arthur slid out of bed one morning onto the floor and pushed in the plug for the heater. The heater was trapped under the bed with Arthurs old shoes so, in desperation, he reached in. As he pulled it out, the wires became detached from the plug.

'Obtuse' thought Arthur, who by now was well conditioned, and pushed the wires firmly back into the small hole at the bottom of the plug before slipping it into the socket. He got up, put on his old shoes, absent-mindedly switched on the light that no longer seemed to work, then went out into the bathroom.

Mrs Eammon McCandless slid out of bed onto the exact spot Arthur had just vacated. Seeing that the heater was plugged in but not working, she touched the switch on its side.

Immediately she found herself immersed in her own worst nightmare. Her arms and legs extended out from her body in acutely perfect angles, her hair stood from her head in equidistant, evenly stranded tufts of equivalent length. Everything about her, from the matching saucers of her eyes, to the perfect 'O' of her mouth, breathed symmetry. The shock of such perfection reeled her away from the heater and across the room. With her right foot jammed firmly into Arthur's oversize, one good left shoe, she caught the bird-cage where it hung suspended from the once thought disused light fitting.

Electricity crackled through her once more, illuminating the smoke from the crisp remains of the parrot dangling from the underside of its perch before flinging her back across the room and through the missing door. As she passed the landing, Arthur's shoe furled unerringly in the detached edge of the stair-carpet, swinging her around in a perfect arc and thence down the stairs, striking each step firmly and resoundingly and as regularly as a chiming clock.

'So you see, Miss Finch,' said Arthur, 'She died from a *peculiar* kind of order. Such an *un*ordered order as to be almost, shall we say... *obtuse.*'

Miss Finch shuffled on the sofa, picked up the dead fly from the carpet by its one intact wing, placed it in a small paper bag she took from her pocket, then put it in her handbag.

Arthur toyed with the sea-jade vase, 'She was a good woman,' he said.

Miss Finch straightened the rug with the toe of her neatly polished shoe, lifted the coffee table back to its feet and plumped up the cushions behind her.

'A good and plentiful woman,' said Arthur, '...and with a passion that I once thought matched my own, but one can certainly tire of that.'

And with an obtuse elbow, he knocked the pink onyx ashtray from the mantel. The combined remains of Mr & Mrs Eammon McCandless (Deceased) drifted like silent smoke towards the lounge carpet. Miss Finch dashed forward with a discarded newspaper and caught them. Gently and reverently she tapped their remains into a sea-jade tulip vase.

'But you,' said Arthur, with a deep and secret smile, 'You, Miss Finch, have *acute possibilities!*'

Seven

For the sake of enlightenment, I have to tell you that my Birthday is Christmas day. This is pertinent to my assumption. (And, some say, it accounts for my *holier than thou* attitude.)

You see, I suppose I'm no different than most kids coming up to the age of seven, a place where I have remained emotionally for the rest of my life. Seven, for me, was the beginning of a voyage of discovery, a discovery that it was alright to think as a child while growing older and keeping that freshness of eye and thought that I'd enjoyed previously.

What changed me was that last Christmas, and my last twenty-four hours as a six-year-old.

We lived in a small mid-terrace house not far from town. There was little room in these houses for anything other than the bare essentials, and therefore very few places to hide anything. Christmas and Birthday presents were easy to discover. This particular Christmas and Birthday I set out to find as many as I could. I found them all, and by shaking the boxes and feeling at the parcels I identified each and every one.

I think you know what's coming now. Christmas morning that year was the most anticlimactic moment I have ever experienced. It changed me forever. Sometimes seven, when you least expect it, can do that to a man...

Seven

The box was a locked wooden casket in the bottom of Timulty's grandfathers chest under a sheaf of old letters and vellum share certificates for Malter's Mill, long since gone and now buried beneath a crumbling swathe of council housing.

Timulty himself hadn't been in this attic since he was a child until your man's death and now here he was all thirty three and feeling seven and delving both arms into the chest with the strength of a Will behind him and all necessary permissions granted. He lifted out the box and showed it to O'Keefe.

'There. There. There it is.'

He shook the box gently in the dust mid-air of the loft. O'Keefe sat at the edge of the ladder with his feet trying to dangle nonchalantly down the hole. His socks showed short and white. He pulled at the knees of his trousers,

'Fine. Fine. Fine box it is and there's no mistake of that.'

Timulty shook the box again. From inside something hard knocked against the dark wood as if it were trying to gain their attention.

'Listen, Pat. Will you just listen?' He shook the box again,

'There. There she is. Do you hear it?'

'What I hear,' said O'Keefe, '...is an old box with an old rattle and nothing but your guesses and suppositions as to what might be in there.'

'You've no soul O'Keefe,' said Timulty, 'I was seven, remember? And at seven a man can see things. Why, a man at seven can tell you the shape and size of all the toys in all the Christmas packages in the world and wake up Christmas morning knowing full well what each and every one contains and still not be disappointed!'

He shook the box. The knock came once more.

'There she is.'

'There she is indeed,' said O'Keefe, dragged and pushed back into seven and finding that the shoes still fit.

'There she is.'

Timulty reached into his pocket and took out a brown paper envelope. He tipped keys out of it onto the plank floor. One of them was small and hollow with a loop twist that had rubbed gently through the brass in places where a finger might fit and wonder.

Timulty's hand went straight to it.

'There she is.'

'Well open it then,' said O'Keefe, as Timulty sat there weighing the key in his hand, 'You've talked of nothing else since the bar and now you sit there like the smile on a pint of good Guinness and with no more brains in your head than when you were seven.'

He sensed Timulty's hesitation, and the reason behind it, 'He's dead, man! He can't come back and flay the hide from you this time. Anyway, it's all yours now. The Will said so.'

Timulty looked up, 'The Will said, 'To my grandson Timulty, there was to be an old chest and all the contents therein.' You know, it's terrible hard to go disturbing another man's memories and keepsakes and somehow it seems even more so now that he's gone, and anyway the Will never said anything about making me responsible for all the things that made him what he was.'

O'Keefe place a hand on the edge of the ladder and shifted around, 'It was implicit. The man knew what was in there. And I think that he knew that you knew or he wouldn't have left it to you and anyway until you open the box we still don't know if you've been right all these years or if you've been carrying around this guilt all that time for the knowledge of what may yet turn out to be no more than a glass paperweight with some old sea anemone frozen deep inside it and knocking like the fury to get out. Do we?'

Timulty fitted the key into the lock. His fingers drifted into the rubbed edges of the twist and turned it, once, then again back.

'It wasn't locked,' he said quietly, the words trembling through held breath. With both thumbs he lifted the edge of the lid and the air inside, the old and dark air from a different kind of town, from a town where Malter's Mill still crushed the dark and roasted grain and filled the gardens and washing lines with a fine musky dust, mixed with the new …the new air that was Timulty, whose breath shuddered out as if it were his last and the devil no more than three paces behind and gaining fast.

He placed the open box on the floor between them.

'There she is.'

'Aye,' said O'Keefe, 'Oh, aye. There she is, right enough.'

He looked suddenly older than his years as if the weight of the box and its contents had dragged his face and his skin downwards until they were too heavy for a smile to bear.

'Oh Timulty! You were right! All these years you were right and you with that secret inside you and how it must have rattled some days like the box when you took it out and only you had the key and you never even shared it with me until right now this very afternoon. What a man you must be! What a soul of discretion!'

Timulty stared into the box as if his soul were being sucked into the dark metal lying there amongst the pristine cuttings from the Tribune and the Herald, crisp and sharp still as the day they were printed, kept here in the dark with Timulty's secret and now…

'Aye,' he said, to no-one or nothing in particular.

'Aye,' said O'Keefe.

They sat there in silence for a moment as the blaze that had been the opening of the box subsided into a worrying glow of acceptance and responsibility.

Then, 'Take it out,' said O'Keefe.

'No,' said Timulty, 'Not yet. I want to be seven a while longer.'

O'Keefe looked at him quizzically.

Timulty smiled, 'I told you O'Keefe. You have no soul.'

He reached into the box and lifted a clipping from beneath the gun. He laid it on the flat of his other palm and read the date on the corner.

'Here Pat, look at this. Fourteenth September, Nineteen Thirty Seven.'

O'Keefe leaned over and they sat on the edge of the hole like two crows on a wire, like they had been through school, like they had been through girls and loud nights in dark street bars and now here in this loft in these memories and it seemed that that was the way of things and rightly so.

'Hey Tim,' breathed O'Keefe, 'This is Antrim. Look, there behind the coffin. There's that bluff of stone that looks like a god's footprint. I'd know it tomorrow as good as today.'

'Conlan,' read Timulty. He sat back into the light, 'Sean Conlan. Suspected informer. Taken from the house and shot in the man's own garden in front of his wife and two daughters. *When will the killing stop?*' it says here,' said Timulty, '...and the Cloth appealed for peace and no retribution.'

'Amen,' said O'Keefe, '...as always.'

He pulled a slip from the small pile of five

'Geraghty. Michael. Twenty seven. Nineteen Forty Two. June, and with the flowers in full bloom too. God, but this place is lovely then.'

'It should be,' said Timulty, 'The soil is turned here like no place else on earth.'

O'Keefe flicked through the remainder

'God, Timulty, but this is sickening. This is a six Guinness pile of paper if ever I saw one in which a man could be drowned by the sorrows of others and limp home maudlin' from the bar.'

Timulty lifted one and held it gently, almost reverently on the flat of his hand.

'February Ninth, Nineteen Fifty Eight. Right here in town. Here, Pat. You may not wish to, but I think you'd better see this. And remember, sometimes wishes can't be obliged by the truth.'

He handed the paper to O'Keefe who took it and read from it as though the ink had been placed there just yesterday when he was seven and watched as the box, the box that had held so many secrets, so many fond and loving knee-cradled secrets and memories was locked and cramped and screwed and lowered and filled and never came back and he knew there was no way it could and now here it was, rearing back up out of the ground at him and roaring in his ears with anger and pain and…

'Grandfer… My Grandfer… God, Timulty. What is this place? A mausoleum of memories? Have we come here for our hopes to die, or is this the day of resurrection when all things become known to man? God, Timulty? What is this?'

Their eyes fastened on the gun as it lay in the box in dark blue steel expectation, and for a time it seemed aware and quiet only because it wanted to be, and would remain so while ever they let it. Then as suddenly as it came, the moment passed. The anguish drained from O'Keefe's face.

'God, Timulty,' he said, 'It was a while ago, wasn't it? I never thought… I never thought I'd feel…'

Timulty placed a hand on his and the silence of the thought behind the gesture soothed away the sting from out of the past and brought him smiling gently back to now and the hopes they'd both had on the way here with windows shushing at their loud voices and curtains flapping like widows weeds in the dark late wonderful warm cold nights of the town.

Timulty lifted up the gun.

O'Keefe shifted nervously at the edge of the hole and seemed to withdraw somewhere deep inside himself as if to stop himself from reaching out and taking the gun from Timulty.

'Be careful, now,' he said.

Timulty smiled and turned the gun in his hands, first this way, then that, feeling the cold hard steel-ness of the thing, the unaccustomed weight now it was out of the box and had become a fact instead of a twenty six year-old supposition.

He pulled back a small slide and the barrel slid out to one side on a hinge as smooth as new silk. He spun it with a thumb. There were seven chambers. Five of them empty and two more filled with the horror and possibilities of newspaper clippings as yet unprinted, just waiting to be read and saved pressed close inside a bible. He closed it quickly and spun the chamber.

'Look!' he said, pointing the gun to his temple, 'This is what Grandfer said they did in the trenches, and sometimes for money and sometimes just for the Hell of it!'

O'Keefe was on him like a shot. Four hands clamped over the gun and they fell back into the dust and the shadows with Timulty laughing like an Irish drain.

O'Keefe screamed at him, 'Don't! For God's Sake Timulty! Not even in jest, man!'

Timulty rolled around, belching out the tension of the last few minutes in great guffaws of laughter and tears that fell squeezed from his eyes held tightly shut in case he saw the true foolishness of the situation and had to take himself in hand before it had all gone.

'I would'na, you fool! You Great Bloody Fool! I would'na!'

He opened then closed his eyes again quickly, 'But you should have seen your face! Christ man, I thought the priest was coming with ten thousand Hail Mary's and you with five minutes to say 'em before the Devil caught up with you.'

Timulty sat up, his shoulders still shaking with great sobbing sighs. O'Keefe took the gun from him. He turned it over until his own fingers closed around the grip and the gun flowed and melted inside his hand until it fitted there as if it had always been… and why worry, it said, when things are in their place and look, it's as easy as pointing with your finger, saying, there, that point there, see?, out there on the horizon. Now follow it along until you meet another man who says that his vision of the world is different than yours and what you can't tell is that both of you are wrong, only you know that he's more wrong than you because he can't be inside of you and he can never know just how right it all feels from inside... and that's what makes him a stranger.

'Jeez, Timulty! The sheer Bloody Hell of the thing!'

'Give it back,' said Timulty, snatching it from O'Keefe's hand where it hung like a leper's stick in his grasp.

And now it was Timulty, tall dark, strutting like a god, pushing, prodding, poking with small lightnings into great matters.

'Ah, Patrick! The sheer Bloody Power of the thing.'

He pushed back his jacket and hooked a thumb inside his braces, 'Look, Pat. Do you see the pose? Sheer bloody John Wayne!'

'Strange,' said O'Keefe, 'You look just like your bloody Grandfer.'

'Strange,' said Timulty, sitting down and shaking his head.

'You know,' said O'Keefe, 'I remember your man sitting up all night with a broody pigeon and the way he held that bird so soft and gentle and the way he stroked her... just like it was a woman's breast all full and nippled and rounded and warm to the forbidden touch.'

'Aye,' said Timulty, remembering.

'Oh aye,' said O'Keefe, remembering.

'Strange,' said O'Keefe.

'Strange,' said Timulty.

'Strange,' said O'Keefe, 'I mean, the way he was.' He shook his head to jar loose the thoughts that were cloying to the inside, giving them voice, 'I mean, a man like that.'

'Grandfer?' said Timulty.

'Yes, your bloody Grandfer! Your bloody Grandfer killed my bloody Grandfer and now that I know it, what the Jeezus am I supposed to do with that?'

'It's in the past,' said Timulty, 'What's in the past can't hurt us.'

'But this is here and now!' screamed O'Keefe, tugging the gun loose from Timulty's hand. It slid into his own hand and tracked towards Timulty.

'Perhaps this is *it*? Is this it, Timulty my fine lad? The day of Retribution with a big R? Where the sins of the fathers come a-visiting on a Sunday when there's nowhere else to go and the churches are empty and the bars not yet open? Come on now Timulty, pick one of the four horsemen and get ready to ride with him into oblivion!'

He levelled the gun at Timulty. Timulty dived and rolled behind the chest, screaming, 'You mad bastard O'Keefe! Put the fuckin' thing down! Sweet Jesus, man. Have you taken leave?'

'No,' said O'Keefe, lowering the gun, 'But I owed you that one.'

He smiled gently, almost to himself, 'But Christ, man. You should'a seen your face.'

Timulty came slowly out from behind the chest, his shoulders hurting from the hit and roll of his panic, all laughter gone from them in the silence that dropped between him and O'Keefe.

'Christ, Timulty,' said O'Keefe, 'Christ.'

'Christ,' said Timulty, 'If ever!'

He took the gun back from where it trembled in O'Keefe's grasp. He sat down at the edge of the hole and dropped the gun into his lap where he looked at it.

'Strange,' he said.

'You're an awful man for 'Strange' these days,' said O'Keefe.

'Strange days,' said Timulty, looking at the gun.

'You'd think that something like this, all hard and cold and sharp corners wouldn't somehow fit quite so well on a man, would you?'

'It's the darkness in it,' said O'Keefe, 'The darkness in the box inside another box and boxed inside are memories that we keep boxed because we like to have the key and only let them out when we know they can't frighten us any more.'

'You're an awful man for boxes these days, O'Keefe. Is it Boxing Day?'

O'Keefe looked across at the gun, nodded, 'It surely isn't Christmas. Perhaps we should put it back?'

'In a while,' said Timulty, picking up the gun, 'In a little while. Tell me about your Grandfer.'

'Oh, maybe there's not much to tell. He died when I was seven,' O'Keefe hung his head a little and turned away from Timulty, '...but then you know that now. I don't remember much. Not really.'

He knew that if Timulty saw his face he would know that he was lying. But that's what friends do and if other friends choose not to see what might be there then that spelled it all out as large and plain as a fresh loaf.

'Let's eat,' O'Keefe said, suddenly hungry, 'Put the bloody thing away and let's go down and stuff ourselves to the gills with food and the fine company of each and the other. Come on Timulty. Come on, lad.'

Timulty's face was dark,

'Tell me about your Grandfer.'

'Oh, let's see,' said O'Keefe, 'He liked to eat. I think I must have inherited his appetite. Let's go downstairs and put heredity to the test. Eh? Timulty?'

Timulty was motionless, 'Tell me about your Grandfer.'

'Jeezus Timulty!' said O'Keefe, 'Stop goin' on about my Grandfer and put that fuckin' thing down and come downstairs because right now you're scaring the shite out of me and I don't like it one little bit and Christ you're a strange bastard tonight!'

'Grandfer!' said Timulty.

'Bastard!' said O'Keefe, 'Let go. Christ man, I was only seven.'

'Only seven! Only seven!' shouted Timulty, 'I told you O'Keefe, you have no soul.'

He stood up and strode around the loft, pointing first at this and then that with the gun, 'Don't you know that seven is *the* age. The age where a man is set like a pattern unbreakable and coming in and going out with all the tides of his life and always, always on the inside, where the plan is, always looking the same, being the same, being... seven.'

'Timulty,' said O'Keefe, 'Come and sit down. Right here. Right here by me. Stop waving that thing around or I'll go down by myself and *then* who cares what happens to you I don't know, for you've made a fair shite of everything else, haven't you?'

Timulty stood in the far corner, his back firmly towards O'Keefe.

O'Keefe patted the floor beside him, 'Where's your wife, eh? She couldn't take it when the darkness took you. Off, off on a cloud somewhere and never came back or even asked you for money, you scared the shite out of her so far.'

'Grandfer,' said Timulty.

'Bastard,' said O'Keefe.

A silence fell between them. The silence of a gun under a closed hammer. Because of the years between them it was oiled and polished and smooth as new silk.

'Timulty,' said O'Keefe at last, his voice scarcely touching the surface of Timulty's thoughts, 'How can I tell you of what were only promises. Promises of things that I was only just beginning to recognize. Things that perhaps were and then again perhaps weren't because they never had the chance to blossom before it was all taken away. I can't even tell you about loss because until now I'd never let it through and for now it's all too new and I haven't made sense of it yet. Timulty, don't ask for the things I don't have. Anything I have is yours. Your Grandfer took the rest and when I see you stood there with that thing looking like the tar and spit of him why, I'm trying hard not to hate you right now, right where you're stood and the only thing that's stopping me is that you're Timulty and not him and I've known you all my life and I know, I know, God help me, I know it wasn't you.'

Timulty ignored him. O'Keefe shrugged his shoulders as if that would slough off all the hurt that today had become in ways that he never knew existed. It didn't work.

'Timulty? Please? Dear God, you're scaring me. Put it down.'

Timulty turned and came to sit by him. He flicked the cylinder of the gun open and shook the contents of one chamber onto the floor. He closed the gun and spun it with his thumb.

'There,' he said, 'It's safe now.'

'I still don't like it,' said O'Keefe.

'It's OK,' said Timulty.

They sat for a moment in a warmer silence, then, 'Pat,' said Timulty, 'I'm sorry about your Grandfer.'

'It's OK,' said O'Keefe, 'I'm sure it wasn't your fault.'

'You know,' said Timulty, 'I used to feel sorry because I had a Grandfer that came round on Sundays and holidays and you didn't.'

'That's OK,' said O'Keefe, 'I wouldn't have swapped. I never liked your Grandfer that much anyway. He had a darkness on him sometimes. Even as a kid, especially as a kid, I could sense that. You know, he even came to the funeral?'

'You know,' said Timulty, 'I think we both lost a Grandfer today.'

'Sad, isn't it?' said O'Keefe.

'Sad,' said Timulty, '…and strange.'

'Awful strange,' said O'Keefe.

'Awful,' said Timulty.

'Strange,' said O'Keefe.

And the laughter grew out of them and swelled until it filled the room and the gaps in their lives that had been left by a man impatient with words and anxious for change in his own time, which of course there never was and perhaps never would be, except that here and now in this room and in these two people there might just be a seed of that newness that was the basis of all decent hopes and wishes. They held each other and rocked with the love and laughter inside of it and them.

'You know, you looked just like him, really,' said O'Keefe.

'Oh yes? And who might that be?' asked Timulty.

'John Bloody Wayne!' said O'Keefe.

Timulty looked at O'Keefe. O'Keefe the short, the blonde, the quick look, 'Alright, James Bloody Cagney. Let's see how you look!'

O'Keefe shrank back as Timulty thrust the gun at him, 'No. No. Jeezus, no.'

'It's OK,' said Timulty, 'Look…'

He pointed the gun into a corner of the loft and looked away despite himself. He squeezed the trigger.

Click.

Click.

Click.

Click.

Click.

Click.

'There now,' said Timulty, 'See! It's quite safe.'

He pushed it back into O'Keefe's hands.

'Go on! Give us your best James Cagney look... Jeezus! Our dog can do better than that! That's it, pretend to shoot me. Ah! That's better. Squeeze the trigger. Come on O'Keefe, don't be afraid, be seven. Remember seven?'

'Oh aye,' said O'Keefe, remembering...

The Daddy Tree

If you stand still long enough, the wind will blow away everything around you, except perhaps for the two footprints where you are stood. Then, when you move, you have nowhere to go. Sometimes that wind has taken away the very earth on which your life depends, the crops that you eat and the blossoms from the trees. Sometimes it steals your soul and, with nothing left to hold you together, it blows you inside out to a place where logic has nothing left to hope for, and a packet of seeds and a drink of water and a sense of injustice may just shed light in the depth of despair.

The Daddy Tree

Maggie stomped about in the cool of the yard. The sun was flat and low and early and the brown dirt swirled and twisted around her skinny, six year-old legs in the mean breeze.

She shook the dust from her hair, 'I want my daddy!'

She threw another stone at the kitchen window where she knew her mother would be, 'I want my daddy!'

Lanny rattled on the window pane with her knuckles.

'Stop that! Y'hear?'

Maggie stomped off to the corner where the old dead tree hung raggedly like a broken doll with all his branches loose and bending down like he was, somehow, listening. Maggie sat down in front of him and began to draw pictures in the dirt with a stick.

'An 'git away from that damn tree!'

Maggie ignored her, then after a while she began to talk. Presently she stood up and pressed a small piece of scribbled notepaper onto a low, dry twig.

'*How many more times?*'

Maggie bent down and picked up two handfuls of the bare earth and threw them toward the house. The wind took it up and whipped it away to the east where it chased the brightening sun across the fields, filling dry ditches with silt and chafing away at the dead soil.

Another stone hit the kitchen window. It broke a filmy web in the corner and chipped the glass.

'I want my daddy!'

The window swung wide into the wind and back, then wide again, 'Get your ass over here right now and don't give me none of your little-miss-lost crap!'

Lanny cupped her long dark hair in one hand and bent over the sink to holler again at her daughter.

'An' your daddy ain't comin' back an' you know that just as well as I do!'

Maggie stamped her feet. She let go the dust she had scooped from the floor and her hands slid down the brown dirt front of her little yellow frock,

'When Daddy was here, we had things to *eat*!'

'Don't tell me what we had when Daddy was here. What we ain't got now is Daddy.'

'You made him go away!'

'No, I didn't, honey.'

'Yes you did!'

Maggie threw a stone as hard as she could at the daddy tree, screamed out, 'Yes-she-did!'

Lanny sank back from the window. Her voice husked soft amongst the rattle of empty pans,

'No, I didn't, honey.'

The next stone flew through the open window and pinged off the crockery on the dresser.

'*Yes you did! Yes you did! Yes you did!*'

Lanny screamed back at the window, 'I can see your daddy right now! Every time I look at you he's lookin' right back at me through them eyes o'yours. Don't you look at me that way! Y'hear?'

'Then where's my breakfast? Huh?'

Maggie's voice tapered off and seemed to flow through the kitchen like the dust on the dry morning air.

'When Daddy was here we had breakfast.'

She stomped off across the yard to the corner of the field where the old tree gnarled up from the ground, said some things to him that Lanny couldn't hear, then stomped back.

Lanny opened the screen door, 'Later, hon. I'll get us somethin'. I promise.'

She smiled across the porch and yard, hoping it would unlock some of the anger she could see there in Maggie, watching her hands.

She held them out empty in front of her, 'Later, hon. I promise.'

Maggie sat down in the dirt and stroked her hands through it, watching it drift down between the gaps in her tiny fingers.

'It on'y needs water. Daddy said, it on'y needs water.'

'Before the water gets to it, hon', sun's bleached it and the winds picked it up an' passed it over to some other poor soul a few hundred miles further east an' all we got left is mud slick as an eight ball. When it rains.'

Lanny picked up a little of the dirt and brought it to her nose.

'See? No smell. Except for the dust. That ain't good. Earth should smell o' somethin'.'

Maggie smacked her hands together and stood up.

'Daddy said he was goin' to get some water and then we'd see. We'd have some left over for flowers an' things, an' a new rabbit.'

She looked over to the corner by the shade end of the porch. There was a half-built cage of sorts and some shallow lines she had scratched in the dirt with a sharp stick.

'An' some seeds. Water an' seeds.'

She looked up as Lanny set down on the board edge by the door.

'Can we get some, mom? From town?'

Lanny held out her arms, 'Come here, hon.'

Maggie folded herself into Lanny's lap. She rubbed at her eyes with dirty brown fists.

'When Daddy brings the water, we'll see. Just like he said.'

Lanny smiled down at her and hugged her.

She hated herself for the rabbit. Maggie thought it had got clean away across the field. Lanny had told her it was just dark chicken and they couldn't afford the white stuff no more. Maggie had spit it out.

She picked her daughter up in her arms, carried her through into the kitchen and set her down at the table.

'Alrighty!' she said. 'What would madam like for breakfast?'

She moved up to the refrigerator and half-opened the door so that Maggie couldn't see in.

Maggie thought for a moment, searching her hunger for something familiar.

'Bacon!' she said, 'With tomatoes and egg!'

Lanny slid her face around the edge of the door so that it was hidden from view. A moment later she popped out again.

'Sorry ma'am, the bacon's clean off the menu.'

Maggie grimaced, 'Just the tomatoes and eggs then.'

Lanny slid her face around the door once more.

'Sorry ma'am, the tomatoes are off too.'

Maggie sighed and cupped her tiny, pointed chin in her hands.

'Just the eggs, then.'

Lanny peered around the door.

'Sorry ma'am…'

'Oh, Mom!' said Maggie, 'Please, let there be an egg. Just one. Make there be an egg. Please?'

Lanny shut the door, one hand behind her back.

'What 'you think I am? A chicken?'

She danced around the end of the kitchen.

'Aaa, cluck cluck cluck, cluck cluck cluck cluck!'

'Aw, mom. Stop it, I'm hungry. Please?'

Lanny stopped. She reached beneath the hem of her heavy print, summer-winter skirt and suddenly, between her slim agile fingers, there spun a single egg.

'Boiled or scrambled, ma'am?'

'Both,' said Maggie.

Maggie finally took the egg scrambled, while Lanny emptied the last of a carton of milk onto a dry crust from the bread bin. Breakfast over, they skivvied the pan and two plates then sat out on the porch. They watched the sun drag itself up into a sky waved and ridged with high cloud blowing itself off into the distance.

'Gonna be dry again,' said Lanny.

Maggie was settling herself down into the wicker porch lounger.

'I wanna sleep,' she said. She rolled back and forth with her eyes held tightly shut.

Lanny reached over and touched her hair, turned some strands around her fingers and watched the sun spark off the gold beneath the dust.

'What happened last night?'

'Couldn't sleep,' sighed Maggie, 'Too hungry. My tummy kept rumbling. It kept me awake.'

Lanny's fingertips touched her forehead. It felt cool.

'That's what it was! An' I'd got to thinkin' it was a truck kept goin' by an' not stoppin'.'

'No, mom. It was the thunder in my tummy. It's what made me angry this morning. It was flashin' and bangin', just like that night out in the field. On'y it was inside. And it hurt more.'

Lanny touched her once more then slowly removed her hand.

'I'm sorry, hon. After today it'll be different. I promise.'

'Is Daddy comin' back? Will he bring the water?'

'No, hon. Daddy's not comin' back. But somethin's gonna change. Something has to change.'

'But without the water, the seeds won't grow. Are we gonna get the seeds today, mom?'

'We'll see,' said Lanny, 'We'll see.'

Maggie drifted off into sleep.

Lanny turned on the water to wash her face. The last of the brown dirt-clogged tank drained into the bowl and stopped. She looked out into the yard where the windmill was rocking in the breeze. The 'foils were broken and lop-sided and it swung at the bottom of an arc, never quite gaining enough momentum to rotate. Henry's idea of mending it had been to knock out a good 'foil opposite the broken ones so as to balance it up. There were now all too few left.

Like the choices in my life, thought Lanny, see-sawin' in the wind and always comin' to rest in the same place.

She looked over to the dresser in the kitchen. She had taken to doing that more often of late. She lifted the key from its hiding place behind the fridge and unlocked the drawer.

Outside, the windmill swung its pendulum arc, ticking in the wind like the clock of all her years. She hardly noticed as her hand slid into the drawer. She pulled it out and held it in the air. Spanning her slim agile fingers, was the bright unforgiving chrome of a gun.

Lanny moved out to the porch and sat down on the tired boards beside the lounger. She flicked over the catch beside the hammer and the cylinder of the revolver slid smoothly out to one side. There was now just the one bullet. It hid beside the five empty chambers like a mouse quivering in a hole and you knew that if you touched it, just so, it would leap and fly and it would be gone. She closed the gun and slid off the safety. With the snub muzzle she lifted some loose strands of hair where they fell across Maggie's eyes, so that she could look at them and see Henry again in the way they rose at the corners, and how there was a crease right there beside the nose that would always be him whenever she looked. She watched as the bright chrome of the gun slid around the dusty blonde hair like the moon behind a cloud. She stroked it down the length of an ear then placed it square against the temple. Her finger stroked the trigger.

At three o'clock that afternoon, Lanny walked in from the outskirts of town. After the two miles from the farm her limbs hung loose in the heat, jangling from her frame. Her head moved like the high clouds, her body as if propelled by the sun at her back and the wind tearing her apart and scuffing in the dust from her dragging feet. She stumbled once, going down on one knee, the dust sticking to the oil on the muzzle of the gun she held in her hand.

The town was quiet. The people out, scattered across the dust trying to stem the tide of the wind and the drought on little dirt farms crouched together around the outskirts as if they were afraid to let go of the town and become something of themselves. Something foreign. Alien even. In a land where things used to grow.

Lanny jolted through the door of Baker's Hardware like she was on a wire. Once inside she leaned, half-fell, against the door. She pressed the side of the gun against her temple, feeling it cold, letting it suck the heat from her brain and body.

Baker ducked behind the counter.

'Hey, Lanny! Be careful, you know, you could kinda...'

The gun wavered in his direction. Lanny braced it with her other hand.

'I want seeds... and water. I want water.'

Baker's wife came through from the back. He shoo-ed her into the storeroom with a swish of his hand. Lanny heard the jangle of a phone from the back room.

'I want seeds...'

'Sure thing, Lanny. Just keep that thing low, willya?'

He moved to the end of the counter.

'Look! I'm comin' around. Takin' it slow, like. I ain't gonna hurt you, Lanny. Give me the gun.'

His hand reached out to take the gun.

'I want seeds.'

Baker backed off from the steel grey in Lanny's eye.

'OK! OK! What kind of seeds? Potatoes? Carrots? Beans?'

'Flowers.'

'Cain't eat flowers, Lanny. Have somethin' that grows. Somethin' you can eat.'

'Cain't grow nothin' you can eat here, 'cept wishes, you know that.'

Lanny moved a step towards him. Her skirt clung to the edge of the door.

'I want flowers. I have a special place to put them. Somewhere I know they'll grow.'

Baker turned and reached down a long dark wooden box. The top was open and Lanny could see that it was filled with packets of flower seeds, their covers bright like cheap curtains. She glanced down at her skirt and tugged it loose from the door.

'You pick some,' she said, the gun never wavering, 'They have to be yellow and pink. And some red. Yes. Some. Bright red…'

She looked at the dust caked on the end of the barrel.

'No. Just the one red.'

Baker carefully selected six packets and laid them on the counter. Their colours burned gaudy and bright against the dark mahogany. Lanny half-smiled but her eyes remained steely and her fingers taut and white.

'How much?'

'They're yours,' said Baker, watching her eyes for that snap that would take her clean over the edge.

'Take' em.'

Lanny's head snapped up,

'How much! I don't take nothin'!'

Baker lifted a catalogue and thumbed the pages. He scribbled nervously on a pad then looked up.

'One dollar, ninety eight cents.'

'And a gallon of branch water. How much is that?'

Baker pulled a clear plastic bottle from the cool cupboard and took to scribbling again.

'Let's see. That's …and for the water…'

He looked up at Lanny.

'Three dollars, fifty six cents.'

Lanny picked up the seeds and tucked them into the pocket of her skirt. She snatched up the water container.

'I'll be back.'

Lanny staggered towards the bank. It sat out across the street in the dust waiting for the boom that never came. Inside, the bank was cool and empty and the gun clattered loudly on the counter as Lanny laid it beside the glass. The cashier turned to look behind her. She was alone.

'Can… can I help you?'

Lanny smiled at her and put down the water bottle. She picked up the gun with both hands and suddenly felt as though a huge bell had tolled between them.

'I want some money.'

'How… how much?'

The barrel of the gun tapped lightly against the edge of the till.

'Three dollars, and fifty six cents.'

The street was empty as Lanny made her way back across to Baker's Hardware. She opened the door and placed the three dollars and fifty six cents on the counter. Moving off up the street she made her way towards the edge of town. In the distance she could hear the wail of sirens and wondered idly where the fire was.

Baker stuck his head out from behind the screen door and waited until Lanny was fifty yards up the street before he ventured fully out. He stood there with the sun at his back and scratched his head, watching her. His wife came out beside him, stooped low, the slab sides of her face between both hands. Baker took a step forward. His wife caught the back of his shirt.

'Don't be foolish. That's a real gun.'

'I ain't foolish, an' I know a gun when I sees one.'

He half-turned and prised her fingers from the damp cloth.

'I think I know a killer when I sees one too. I just wanna find out.'

As they passed along the street, the store-fronts opened wide like windows on a hot summer's noon.

On the edge of town, where the main street crossed the highway, two black-and-whites were drawn up in a chevron.

Lanny jangled her way towards them towing a small arrowhead of townspeople. As she approached the cars, a man stepped out. He waited until she drew close.

'Lanny?'

Lanny smiled absently to herself and kept on walking.

He fell in beside her. 'Lanny?'

Lanny squinted up at the sky.

'It's gonna be hot,' she said, and walked right on through the gap between the cars. The sheriff stopped, watching her walk away.

Baker took his arm. 'Come on. We gotta see this.'

The sheriff took off his hat and brushed away some of the dust settled on his shirt.

'She rob your store?'

'Yes!' said Baker, 'Hell, No! No. She paid for everythin'.'

'Then what's your problem?'

'She had a gun. Pointed it right at me!'

The sheriff replaced his hat.

'The gun I can take care of. You go back and mind your store. Folks're hungry around here.'

He pointed to the cashier.

'You from the Bank?'

The cashier nodded.

'New, aren't ya?' said the sheriff.

The cashier nodded again. 'I been around three, nearly four months. Since I got married.' She held up the ring.

'Nice,' said the sheriff, 'You handle the mortgages?'

The cashier hid the ring with her other hand.

'Some.'

'Lanny's?'

'Yes.'

The sheriff turned to watch Lanny receding slowly into the pale distance.

'How much she owe?'

'Can't tell you that.'

The sheriff fixed her with a look.

The cashier twisted hard on the ring.

'She's paid off half the loan and still owes 'bout four times what it's worth. Same as the rest around here.'

'How much'd she take?'

'Three dollars, fifty six cents.'

'Put it on her mortgage.'

The sheriff drew a line in the dust with the toe of his boot.

'Now go on home.'

He followed Lanny the last mile or so up to the house.

The porch door banged fitfully in the wind. The sheriff came out of the house and dropped the latch to secure it. The house had been ghost empty. Lanny was out in the yard on her knees over by the back corner where the earth was darker. The gun lay in the dirt beside her feet. Using both hands she drew a sharp stick across the soil. The sheriff watched as the scratches grew deeper and darker. She took the flowered packets from her skirt pocket and placed the seeds carefully in small holes she made with her finger at the bottom of the scratches, then just as carefully covered them over with the dust. She took the top from the bottle of water and poured it sparingly along the lines until none was left. The sheriff took off his hat and covered his right hand with it.

'Lanny?'

Lanny's head dropped forwards an inch.

'Sheriff.'

The sheriff moved a little closer.

'The gun, Lanny. Give me the gun.'

Lanny turned her head around.

'Sure.'

She tossed the gun into the dirt by his feet. He picked it up and flicked open the chamber.

'The bullets, Lanny. Where are the bullets?'

'Never had but two,' she said.

She smiled up at him as her face creased with a slow dream of a smile and her eyes filled with all of the rain inside.

The sheriff flicked back the cylinder and slipped on the safety. He slid the gun into a hip pocket and put back his hat against the sun.

'Where's Maggie?'

Lanny brushed her hands together and shook the dirt back where it belonged,

'Oh, she's probl'y talkin' to her daddy 'bout right now.'

'How'd you mean?'

'Oh, bit of this, bit of that. How mean I am. Things I make her do. How I don't give her nothin'.'

'Lanny, where is she?'

Lanny drew the stick through the dark soil again. The groove was deep but the dirt just ploughed back in.

'Out on the corner, by the old tree.'

She placed her hands behind her in the dirt and shook out her dark brown hair.

'Thinks it can talk to her daddy. He once told her it could, that it was magic. Leaves messages to him all th' time. Been there most th' day.'

The sheriff stepped sideways to where he could see Maggie sat out in the dirt field talking away and beating the dust with a switch. Around her, where the parched boughs of the tree swept close to the earth, they bloomed, each twig and branch heavy with a blossom of white paper.

The Seaside Things

Like most people of my age, I have had the misfortune to be present at the point of death of people who were very close to me, and those experiences left me with an unanswerable question. How to explain the moments of lucidity that can appear immediately prior to the loss of all bodily function.

These moments have sometimes taken the form of one-sided conversations with loved ones who have passed previously. I have no answer for this, but having seen it in action I have tried to come up with an explanation that I can live with. This story is about just that scenario.

The story also concerns the way that bereavement affects the ones left behind, after all, they are the ones who are acutely aware that you are dead while, mercifully, you are in blessed oblivion.

I have known people enshrine the life, and indeed the very belongings, of those who have departed their lives, effectively building a wall between themselves and a continuing reality, espousing a kind of stasis in which nothing moves or changes.

From this stasis, feeding initially on itself and a situation frozen eternally in time, comes a sense of blame. Blame is a ravenous creature. It feeds on 'what if', not on 'what is'.

And eventually on you.

The Seaside Things

With her hands immersed in soft suds and the pale delicacy of china, Hattie felt the switch go over in her head.

She recognized it instantly. Her mother had described it so perfectly, she didn't even think to panic. Instead, a slow smile spread across half her face. It was like opening the door to find an old friend you'd been expecting for years.

She tried to open the drawer to trap the tea-towel in the edge but her left arm wouldn't lift. She folded the towel one-handed and draped it on the radiator, then found the sudden inspiration to turn on the tap before fetching the kettle. She filled it through the spout and placed it on the hob… then stopped for a moment to work out how to strike a match.

The box jammed itself neatly between the cooker and the edge of the sink unit with the sandpaper edge face up. This isn't going to be so hard, she thought, sitting down to wait for the kettle, and all the while reorganizing the kitchen in her head. She lifted her useless left hand into her lap and chafed the scar tissue gently with her right, then placed it into the pocket of her pinafore where it would stay out of trouble.

Things would just take a little longer now, that's all.

Before she lifted the boiling kettle she drew back the net curtain to peer out into the street, something she hadn't felt comfortable with for as long as she could remember. Traffic skimmed past on the wet tarmac scarcely thirty feet from her door. The sun was beginning to show and water steamed along the gutters, filling the air with ephemeral wisps. Two cars approached from different ends of the street and she watched calmly as they passed safely in front of her. This was new... and perhaps welcome.

That same late August afternoon, with the sun now a solid pole through the glazed south-light and the sound of a trapped bee sawing away in a corner and her left leg dragging behind her, no more use than a prop, Hattie climbed the steps into the loft. She made her way under the eaves and with great effort single-handedly dragged out the trunk that she and the policeman had wrestled into there some forty-odd years ago.

The travel trunk was small but capacious and patterned with hide as softly grained as the skin of her good right hand, and its black, half-dome lid had remained closed for all that time since it had been ripped from the boot-rack of the car.

Stripping open the buckles, Hattie pushed back the lid. She held her breath for what seemed an age, then reached in and took out the seaside things. The sand-coloured blanket she shook open onto the floor, then lifted out a brightly-striped beach bag. Underneath it was a small collapsible deck chair. Hattie struggled this open and placed it on the blanket.

Tipping out the contents of the beach bag, she sat down amongst them and picked up the old camera. She peered into the view-finder, shading the bright glass cube from the sunlight. Out in the distance across her own private beach was a small figure, upside down and waving. Hattie looked up suddenly, then guessed she must have seen her own toes, wriggling their way down into the sandy blanket. Her heart leaped at the small moment it had given her.

Placing the camera carefully on the floor beside her, Hattie climbed into the deck chair and picked up a large pink shell. Cupping it to her ear she heard the sound of a gently turning sea, very far away. If she were to stay up here listening to the sea amongst these long-ago but seldom-forgotten things, who would notice? After all, it was her fault there was no-one left to care. Seconds later she was asleep.

She awoke at ten minutes to four as a shadow lingered between herself and the sun. She tidied the things back into the trunk and made her way downstairs.

After a few days, the only place where Hattie felt alive was in the loft. The rest of the house was becoming dark and indistinct as if little existed below the old wooden steps that led up to her own patch of sea-side. In Hattie's sea-side the sun always shone, the air was always still and calm and the sand warm between her toes. And while she slept up there, there was no sound of rending metal to fill the dreaming-time.

After the heat of August had passed, the following week drew in September storms to drum the cumulus sky amid lightnings and great volumes of tumbling air. For four days the air in the loft shook and crashed.

For those four days Hattie stayed away, but by the fifth she found she could resist no longer. With a last look beyond the landing window at the rain driving away towards the east, she went up into the loft.

As her head cleared the hatch the storm broached the horizon and a watery sun split the raindrops on the south-light into shifting, cathedral sparks. Taking out the seaside things she set them down carefully. She unfolded the deck chair that now seemed drab against this light and sat down.

Within reach at the bottom of the trunk was a small brass telescope, hardly bigger than an opera glass. She picked it up and held it into the stream of light. Looking through it she could see her toes, then her eye moved upwards to the place where the sand seemed to run out forever towards a thin line of blue at the edge of the world... where a small figure stood, watching her.

She dropped the glass into her lap and the loft rushed back in to trap her in its drowning kaleidoscope. The sun was growing stronger now and the pitter-patter roof tiles were becoming silent. Wriggling her toes deeper into the softness of the blanket, Hattie stole the quiet song of the sea from within the fragile shell and dropped quietly off to sleep.

At ten minutes to four she awoke, having dreamed that someone called her name.

The next day was fine and Hattie drew herself up into the loft filled with anticipation for its warmth. The sun, brandishing light fiercely as a deep golden bar, pillared the south-light; pounding its way amongst cracks and shakes in the floorboards. Dust motes flowed its length, swept along in the river of light. Pulling the deck chair into its midst Hattie allowed the sun to splash around her, reflecting from her skin back up into the dark timbers of the roof. Closing her eyes, she held the shell to her ear and drifted into sleep.

In that sleep her eyelids became heavy, as if the light against which they were now lifting pressed down upon them with all the weight of the sun. Her lips rimed with the tart of sharp salts and air that brushed crisp and lightly across her nose. Slowly, her eyes began to discern the shape of a small figure out across the beach. The figure raised its hand and began to beckon. Above the hush of the waves came the sound of his words.

'Hattie! Hattie!', and the striking of the sea far away across the sand.

She awoke at ten minutes to four, remembering that someone called her name.

The dreams became a curiosity to Hattie, but no more than that. The real puzzle was why she hadn't dreamed them before but, like the switch in her head, she had welcomed them. All she did know was that they drew her into the loft, and from there into a deeper, quieter sleep than any within memory.

As she slept, her toes buried deep in the pale sanded wool of the blanket, the sun passed behind a cloud and the heat of the loft began to fade. It fell by degrees until Hattie gave an involuntary shiver in her sleep. She turned in the deck chair to curve herself against the sail of canvas and felt the edge of a travel rug slip against her shoulder. Without thinking she pulled it up to cover the exposed side of her neck, then stopped. Slowly her eyes opened and examined the bound edge of the rug. It was soft and deep with recognised tartan reds and greens. She looked up and out towards the horizon where, in the distance, a small figure waved and shouted.

Although the voice was indistinct, she thought it said,

'Hattie! Oh, Hattie! The shells, Hattie! The shells!'

Her eye caught a movement that turned her face along the shore. Beside her chair was a man, willowy tall and slender, skin taut and glowing darkly with sun. He leaned slightly, his back toward her, sheltering her from the breeze while small unconscious movements rippled the snake of his spine, coiling beneath the warm sand of his skin. His hair blew night-dark in the wind that sprang suddenly from offshore, bringing with it a scent and the sound of the sea. Drifting far overhead, a white bird clippered the wind in silence. Curiously satisfied, Hattie fell back into the warmth of sleep.

At ten minutes to four she awoke, having dreamed of Michael.

By early October the sun was ready to leave the loft and Hattie had felt several other but smaller switches turn over in her head until the left side of her body had become little more than a distraction. The late autumn sun burned slow and fat on the horizon and now only poked around in the dust beneath the south-light for an hour or two, where Hattie waited to feel its warmth.

One clear afternoon, while the jet stream shredded the high cirrus into ragged, deepest pink, Hattie made her way into the loft and again set out the seaside things. Under the eaves the gutters hustled with dried leaves, patterning the tiles with the faint scratch of driven sand on driftwood. She sat with the shells in her lap, turning each one in her hand and was surprised at the small, gritty, graininess of them. Smiling self-consciously, she remembered the places from where they'd been taken and wrapped for the journey in paper tissue as if they had been precious stones.

In those few sleepy moments, Hattie began to understand just how alone she'd been for the last forty years, and found time to consider that perhaps that's what she'd deserved. She *had* insisted on driving home.

She sat up abruptly as a final switch was thrown in her head. The thought came that she was dying… she held it for a moment... for the first time ever without fear or pain. She sat back into the chair and relaxed her body completely.

Without warning, the forbidden memory played in her head like a monochrome film complete with grain and scratch.

She watched the lorry come towards her safely then... suddenly... veer across the road until the world turned black.

She reached down into the seaside trunk and took out the shattered wristwatch she had been unable to let herself see before. The case and strap stained black with blood, the glass badly broken and pushed into the dial, stopping the hands forever at ten minutes to four.

She strapped it onto her dead left wrist and the loft exploded into a scald of boiling water on her skin, an overwhelming stench of steam and petrol and hot oil pouring through where the windshield had been, where a large shard of it was deeply embedded into the left side of her face.

With her one good eye she saw the shape of Michael thrown through the windscreen and draped across the bonnet by the impact, his head at an acute angle, his perfect black hair shredded and tangled, and remembered noticing that his shoes were ready for heeling.

She looked down to see the metal of the dashboard split and ripped into the large, hard protrusion of her belly, blood and water flowing copiously from between her legs, mixing with the other broken fluids to connect her indelibly with the machine.

Above her head the shattered battery swung from its connecting wires, raining acid down the side of her face and body.

Hattie had insisted on two separate funerals.

She calmed her breathing and the world snapped back to a closer horizon where the sun streamed flat, low and orange through the raised dust of the loft. She again picked up the shells and held them to her ear as they fastened her once more soundly to sleep.

After what seemed an age, Hattie awoke to the delicious tang of a clear sea and the gentle wings of a sun-warmed breeze against her cheek. Although her eyes were closed she was aware of someone standing by the chair. She relaxed the taut muscles of her face and eased her eyes into the brightness of an afternoon sun. The shadows cut long, hard and clean across a beach. Before her was a small boy. He was entirely naked and his hair was tousled, recently wet and now drying, salt licks crystallising slowly amidst a deeper brown. His eyes watched her hands where they rested in her lap amongst moist, fresh, shells. Behind him, white birds noisily crowded something pale at the edge of the water.

As the boy spoke there was a hushed urgency in his voice, his eyes now bright with a fresh smile, his gaze lifted somewhere beyond Hattie's head.

'Dad! She's here.'

From behind her, Hattie became aware of a soft footfall in the sand. The man came around to face her and she could see at once that he was the boy, but grown over like the rings of a tree and that the soft wind on the salt air edged at the timbre of his voice.

'Hello,' he said, 'We've been waiting for you.'

Hattie looked up into his eyes.

'I'm sorry,' she said, feeling the loft fade into the sound of her words.

Michael smiled down at her, 'It wasn't your fault.'

His sun-drenched fingers struck gentle patterns along the salt-bleached frame of her chair; his skin shone dark from every stroke of light.

'We brought you down by the sea each bright afternoon.'

Reflected in his eyes Hattie could see the chapel beyond the estuary dunes and the fingers of its tower clock, poised at ten minutes to four.

He placed a hand on the shoulder of the boy. His eyes lifted with the colours of the sea and a smile rode the tides of his face.

'Harry wouldn't give up. He knew that the shells would bring you.'

Hattie watched the boy who held out his own sand-sifted fingers.

'*Harry?*' She turned to Michael, '*This is… Harry?*'

'Yes,' he said, '…and you're tired, but this time the shells will hold you. Just remember the shells.'

She tried to lift her hands to meet the boy's but they fell away. The shells within her fingers, tumbling carelessly in their browns, pinks and tortoiseshell, spilled unnoticed across her lap and onto the blanket.

Her eyes turned dark as they lost the sun.

Far overhead a white bird called once, then was silenced.

Bananas

Having written Vayu Manush (The Wind Man) I became enamoured of the characters and their quirky localised rivalry. I wanted to write another story that encapsulated these things I had discovered about them during the writing. I hope I did that, and if I did, that it's in a slightly different way, showing a different side to their characters.

It was only when I began to write this that I realised what a tightly drawn circle I'd used to encompass their lives and how narrow I had made their horizons. I had to comfort myself by acknowledging that some people are happy with their lot, however restricted it may seem from the outside, and that repetition can be comforting in that there are few things that can leap out and surprise you... however, sometimes that stability hangs in the balance...

Bananas

Khalil led the oxen slowly out into the roadway and the cartwheels dropped into the ancient ruts with a satisfying creak.

He held his breath for a moment as the mound of green bananas piled high above the cart swayed and settled without disgorging themselves onto the roadside. A huge sigh of relief welled inside him.

Climbing up onto the front of the cart, he felt the seat hard and worn beneath the thin bleached cotton of his kameez. He twitched the ears of the oxen with a long slender pole that held a short whip-cord at the end. First one wheel turned, then the other. The cart shook and rumbled, crushing beneath its iron rims the fallen leaves that lay in the ruts, releasing their sharp scent of autumn into the still air. By the time the cart had been in motion for five minutes, Khalil was asleep, dreaming of their harvest earlier in the day...

'Quickly!' said Gupta, 'Take the seat.'

The loop of rope passed over the top of the tree and as they pulled hard on it, the bottom of the loop hung close to the ground. Bhopal lowered his huge bulk onto the short plank that had been slung into it.

Gupta, along with his and Bhopal's wife, let go of the ropes they had used to bend the tree. Bhopal's feet lifted slightly and hovered over the dusty ground. The tree attempted to raise its head back to the sky, but the bunched bananas remained hanging like greenly glowing lanterns close by their heads.

Khalil's wife took the pole with the hooked blade nailed securely to the end and cut one bunch loose from the tree. Gupta lowered it as gently as he could to the ground. Bhopal's feet lifted six inches into the air.

'I will need more weight,' he said, 'Wife!'

'There is no room on the seat for me,' said his wife, 'How should I sit?'

'Perhaps I should be the one on the seat,' said Gupta, '…then there would be room for the two of us if we held each other tight.'

The blunt end of a pole caught him squarely behind the ear. He looked around in dismay.

'I am sorry,' said his wife, 'I was not looking. *Only listening…*' she added, so that only Gupta could hear.

She cut another bunch loose with the lance. It took Gupta unawares and carried him with it to the ground. Bhopal lifted eighteen inches as the weight dropped from the tree.

'Aleh!' he shouted, 'Wife!'

His wife came up from behind and placed one foot beside him on the seat. She grasped the rope with each hand and stood up inside the loop. They settled a further six inches back towards the ground.

'Wife,' said Bhopal, 'You need more weight. Do I not feed you well?'

'Yes, my Husband,' she replied, 'You feed me well but work me better. The weight follows me around but I am never still long enough for it to catch up.'

Gupta's wife cut loose another bunch. It hit Gupta as he was getting up from the floor. Bhopal and his wife rose another foot into the air.

'Aleh!' they said.

'Be quiet,' said Gupta, 'Might I remind you whose idea this was?'

His wife cut loose another bunch. Gupta wrestled it slowly to the floor. Bhopal and his wife began to sway with the bouncing motion of the tree, their combined weight travelling up and down, four feet above the ground.

'Aleh!' shouted Bhopal. The birds lifted from the treetops around the plantation, no longer curious, but anticipating disaster with each cry. Their wings filled the air with the sound of a sudden shower of rain. Khalil's wife jumped up and grasped the seat, adding her weight to that already on it.

Slowly, the seat returned to the floor.

'Thank you,' said Bhopal, 'I retract every statement I have ever made about your husband.'

Khalil's wife made as if to let go of the rope. The seat bucked and swayed threateningly.

'I see now,' said Bhopal, quickly, '...from where he obtains his eminent good sense and wisdom. Every man should have such a wife.'

Khalil's wife took a firmer grip upon the rope. The seat steadied, six inches from the ground. At which point, Bhopal's wife got off. The seat shot up in an instant to six feet, then settled back towards the dusty soil.

'And what is wrong with the wife you already have?' she asked.

'Nothing. Nothing,' said Bhopal, panic appearing as a wavering edge in his voice.

Gupta's wife cut loose another bunch of bananas. This time, Gupta was ready. He spun them on his hip as they fell and placed them directly on the growing pile. Bhopal shot up another two feet but his voice rose a full octave.

'I only meant that, as I am the only man who can experience such wifely perfection as yourself, then every other man deserves at least a woman with such ineffable common sense as is possessed by the wife of Khalil.'

Seeing the look on his wife's face, and realising in an instant that she remained unconvinced, he added…

'And even this can only ever be second best to one such as yourself.'

'If I am to be only second best,' said the wife of Khalil, '…then I am unfit to hold a position that should be occupied by the perfection of your wife.'

She let go of the rope and dropped to the floor. Bhopal, unaccompanied, shot ten feet into the air then settled back to six.

'Aleh!' he said, watching the ground approach and recede between his feet. Gupta's wife extended the pole as far as it would reach and trimmed the last bunch. Gupta spun it deftly onto the pile as Bhopal shot up and bounced a further four feet from the ground.

'Get me down!' he shouted. They stood beneath him, looking up at the soles of his feet where they twitched in panic.

'You cannot leave me here,' he said.

'Then please instruct us,' said Gupta, with no discernible trace of a smile, '…as to how this shall be accomplished.'

'I don't know,' said Bhopal, '*You* must think of something.'

'May I remind you again,' replied Gupta, '…whose idea this was.'

Bhopal remained silent, studying their eyes as they gazed up at him from the safety and permanence of the floor.

'And as with all good ideas,' continued Gupta, '…one should follow them through.'

He shrugged his shoulders and made to walk away, then stopped and turned.

'So when you have found the solution, if you will be so good as to shout, then we will hear you and return.'

Bhopal raised his eyes to the heavens.

'Are these my friends?' he shouted, 'Are these the people whose lives I have altered irrevocably with my own brain? With my own ideas and devices for the saving of needless labour and the fruitless consumption of energy?'

'Like working your wife half to death?' asked Khalil's wife.

Down below, heads nodded in swift agreement.

'Like the water-driven heat extractor that works only during the three hottest months of the year?' asked Gupta.

The women laughed mercilessly.

'I agree that some things may require a little more thought,' said Bhopal, '…but my brain works tirelessly towards the solution of life's problems so that we may all eventually benefit therefrom.'

Gupta smiled broadly, the corners of his mouth etched deep and curved as the bananas laid in a large pile on the ground.

'Then we await your wisdom,' he said.

'Wife!' shouted Bhopal.

'I am sorry,' she replied, 'But my perfection hides a certain modesty by which it would be unthinkable that I could presume to have a solution to a problem that my husband was unable to find.'

'And my common sense,' said Khalil's wife, '...reminds me that no-one is better placed to resolve a problem than the person most directly experiencing it.'

'And *I* think,' said Gupta's wife, '...that I do my most constructive thinking when my hands are busily preparing food, a task they seem to do endlessly and without assistance.'

She looked hard at Gupta, who allowed his gaze to switch only between Bhopal's feet and the bananas.

'I think a little tea, taken while Bhopal continues his internal struggle with Life's machinations, would be appropriate at this time,' she said.

'That sounds to me,' said Khalil's wife, '...like common sense.'

'Perfect,' said Bhopal's wife.

Gupta followed them out of the clearing, deflecting Bhopal's cries as easily from his shoulders as if they were so many bananas.

Khalil awoke with the scent of salt sharp in his nostrils. His eyes opened slowly to see the figure of Marunesh seated in his large brass chair at the end of the jetty. Beside him, a boat rocked gently in the water as the small waves touched and tipped its underside. The boat was half full of firm green bananas and the jetty creaked and moved as the hardwood gunwales pressed against it with the movement of the water.

The oxen had stopped just short of the jetty, at the point where the rutted track ended.

Marunesh waved to him.

274

'So. You have returned at last. And how was the land of departed spirits?'

Khalil looked up quizzically, shading his eyes from the reflected sunlight. Marunesh took a large silver watch from a pocket sewn to the outside of his robe.

'Your oxen arrived here an hour ago,' he said, 'I have been waiting since then for the rest of your senses to catch up.'

'Why did you not wake me?' shouted Khalil.

'I know of your wife and her beauty,' said Marunesh, 'A man with a woman such as her gets so little time for rest.'

He slid the watch back into its pocket, 'I found room in my heart for a little pity. So I let you sleep.'

Khalil felt his face flush with anger, then realised that this anger exposed would weaken his bargaining position, and that this was exactly what Marunesh had intended.

He climbed unsteadily from the cart and took hold of the harnesses. Turning the oxen right around, he backed them and the cart out onto the jetty. The oxen felt the timbers move beneath their feet and set up a deep, mournful lowing. Their hooves chattered the wood nervously in fear.

Marunesh sat smugly in his deep brass chair. Beside it was an ornate stand perhaps six feet high, also in brass, to the top of which was attached a strong arm that pivoted in the middle. A chain was attached to each end of this arm. One of the chains attached to an arrangement of rods above the chair, the other to a similar arrangement above a huge brass pan.

Khalil stared at Marunesh in dismay.

'It would seem that Life has been good to you, Marunesh,' he said, 'For you have become much heavier than you were last year.'

'Ah, yes,' replied Marunesh, '...but the deal is still the same. For my bodyweight in bananas, you shall receive your ten rupees.'

'But this time,' said Khalil, '...you appear much heavier than the last. And the time before that too.'

'That may be so,' said Marunesh, '...but is the world not filled with troubles?'

Khalil waited for the explanation that he knew would follow and also that it would make no real sense, yet would retain, for him, an indefinable and indestructible logic.

'And from all these troubles,' continued Marunesh, '...do I not protect you?'

He shifted his huge bulk in the seat. The scales creaked their brass joints and clattered their open plates and chains,

'Do I not,' he said, '...in spite of all the changes in the world beyond our control, maintain the price at ten rupees for my bodyweight in bananas?'

'But this time,' replied Khalil, '...you are so much heavier. And it now takes more bananas to achieve the ten rupees. This is hardly fair.'

'This is a thing called inflation,' said Marunesh, 'It is a phenomenon with which the western world is most familiar and unfortunately, as is the way of most things in this world, it has found the time to work its way around to us.'

'Then how have I not heard of this thing before?' asked Khalil.

'It is the measure of my protection,' replied Marunesh, '...that you remain blissfully unaware and untroubled of mind so that you may sleep peacefully. As has just been demonstrated beyond question.'

Khalil reluctantly hefted the first bunch of bananas into the pan and the chains took up the slack. The chair moved not one fraction. By the time the cart was half emptied, Marunesh lifted silently and gracefully into the air. Khalil stopped and wiped his brow.

'One more,' said Marunesh.

'No,' said Khalil, 'That is enough. I have lifted you from the floor by your own, not inconsiderable, weight in bananas.'

'I have not yet achieved the point of balance,' said Marunesh, indicating with his hand the discrepancy between the height of the pan and the base of the chair.

'It is enough, in my opinion,' said Khalil.

'Then let us consider opinions,' said Marunesh, 'Whilst I am given time to ponder, I am beginning to form an opinion as to the condition and ripeness of these bananas. It may be they have been on the tree too long.'

He pulled a banana from the closest bunch and peeled back the skin. He tasted it with the tip of his tongue before swallowing half of it in an instant. His eyes closed and he ruminated for a moment, the taste still fresh within his mouth,

'It may be,' he said, '…that by the time I have crossed the bay, these will have yellowed and become fully ripe. What shall I do with them then? Feed the fishes?'

Khalil threw another bunch onto the scales. Marunesh shot upwards in delight as the scales hit the stop. He put up a hand.

'That will do,' he said. 'Now, please stack them carefully on the boat.'

Khalil looked around in surprise, noticing for the first time an otherwise obvious absence.

'Where is Mangla?'

'I could no longer afford to pay him,' said Marunesh, 'Inflation being what it is.'

'Then who shall load them?' asked Khalil.

Marunesh smiled, his eyes alight with the sweetness of the victory within his grasp.

'You can always put them back on the cart,' he said, '...and upon your return give my regards to Gupta the Pig.'

Khalil stared into the eyes of the village oxen. Their black depths swallowed him in their look of despair and lack of choice. He was here to represent the village... but what if he went back empty-handed and the crop rotted on the cart...

He stacked the first bunch onto the boat, remembering the laughter in their faces at the harvest only that morning.

'How long has he been there?' asked Gupta.

'Three cups of tea each,' replied his wife, '...and an eternity of listening to his cries.'

Bhopal's wife put down her teacup.

'He was becoming most constructive in his criticisms for a while. But, alas, he seems to have returned to his normal level of husbandly abuse. I shall no doubt be found responsible for the whole situation,' she said.

'I would remind him of your perfection, if that were to be the case,' said Gupta. His teacup hid the brightness of his smile.

'I myself was the subject of the most inventive remarks.'

He held out the tea cup to be filled afresh.

'He derived a strange equation between weight,' he looked down at his own spindly arms and legs, '...and the possession of common sense and integrity. It seems,' he went on, '...that my lack of bulk precludes the possession of an imagination and an ability to observe and resolve the truth in all or any given situations.'

'I am sure he did not mean to be so cruel,' said Bhopal's wife, a note of sarcasm adding a mocking tone to her words, 'He is angry at himself. He would not wish to offend you, I am sure.'

'On the contrary,' said Gupta, 'I find that I am most happy to accept his observation of my situation, especially, as I told him at the time, it emanates from a loftier perspective than my own.'

'What shall we do with him?' asked Khalil's wife.

Gupta's wife held up the teapot.

'Tea?' she said.

'That makes sense to me,' said Khalil's wife.

Bhopal's wife listened for a moment to the cries as they rose and fell in cadence by scales and degrees of vituperation through the dark-leafed trees between them and the clearing.

'Ineffable,' she said.

'And who am I to comment,' said Gupta, '…upon such perfection.'

Khalil fed the oxen in the yard outside, hiding his face behind the small sacks as he spilled them on the ground.

'18 rupees!' shouted Gupta from the shade of the porch, 'It was worth forty if any at all.'

He threw the coins upon the table where they spun and flashed like wind-chimes in the light shattering through the porch roof.

'The deal was the same,' said Khalil, 'Marunesh's body weight in bananas makes ten rupees.'

'Last year a load like that made thirty,' said his wife. 'How is it different this year?'

'It is Marunesh himself,' replied Khalil, 'This year he seems so much bigger than last.'

'Then he should pay us more for his bodyweight, if that is the case,' said Gupta. A slight breeze drifted Bhopal's cries through the thin edge of forest behind the house.

'What is that noise?' asked Khalil.

'It is nothing,' said Gupta. 'It is no more than a problem looking for its own solution.'

Khalil looked puzzled for a moment, then carried on.

'Marunesh says that it is a thing called Inflation. From which he in his mercy protects us.'

'Inflation,' said Gupta, he allowed the word to roll upon his tongue for a moment, waiting for the taste of it to tell him the true meaning hidden within the letters.

'I know of only two things that suffer inflation,' said Khalil's wife from behind them. She stood in the doorway bearing a fresh pot of tea and two cups.

'That is the space between my husband's ears and Bhopal's opinion of himself.'

'Where is Bhopal?' asked Khalil.

Gupta was silent for a moment, then as the breeze caught and filtered the noise from the clearing once more, he indicated the source with a brief nod of his head.

'Ah!' said Khalil, not knowing exactly why he had said it, but knowing all the same that if Bhopal was involved it would entail much noise from him and a corresponding amount of effort by others.

'There must be great works afoot,' he said.

The crescent moon of Gupta's smile lit the shaded heat of the porch.

'More like, ten feet,' he said.

'In the morning,' said Khalil's wife, 'I will take the next load to Marunesh.'

'I will not hear of it!' said Khalil, 'It is not seemly that my wife should do this thing alone.'

'Is it seemly that we should live on 18 rupees when forty are available?' she replied.

Khalil rose from his chair to stand by the circular bamboo table in the middle of Gupta's house. The tea things chimed gently to themselves as he struck the table with the edge of his hand.

'I will not hear of it!' he said.

'Then I will go myself,' said Gupta.

'You cannot,' said his wife, 'You know Marunesh will not deal with you since you insulted his brother.'

'I was twelve,' said Gupta, 'Surely he has forgotten by now? And anyway I was right. His brother was a fat pig.'

Khalil shook his head, 'He mentions it to this day.'

'Still is a fat pig,' said Gupta.

Khalil's wife flicked the ears of the oxen with the whip. They lowed in deep protestation then picked up their pace. She lifted her head and felt the sunlight walk dappled across her face as it slipped from the leaves of the banyan and jackfruit overhead.

There was an undeniable yet indefinable sweetness to the air. The only noise came from the creak of the wheels and the steady huffing sound of the breath steaming in and out of the oxen. She savoured the taste of something on her tongue, then recognised it for what it was, freedom, and behind that a softer taste, hiding almost within the freedom and somewhere behind the responsibility she had been given, of small victory.

Although it was still early, Marunesh's boat was nearly full. Khalil's wife descended gracefully from the cart and backed the oxen expertly along the jetty. Marunesh's eyelids, behind which he had been dozing in the gentle early light, opened and recognised the cart swaying towards him.

'You are almost too late, Khalil,' he said, then added maliciously, 'As you are for most things.'

Khalil's wife came around the rear of the cart and stood silently in front of him. Marunesh almost lifted from his chair in shock.

'Raschida!'

He looked around the cart to see where Khalil was hiding.

'I am alone,' she said.

Marunesh smiled.

'Then you have come at last,' he said, '…to fill the boat of my heart. To usher in the completeness of my life by the addition of your load to mine so that we may sail together, forever fully laden and in profit.'

'I had thought as much at one time in my life, but now…' she looked him up and down, assessing his bulk with an obvious eye.

'But we were promised as children,' said Marunesh, '…and I still await the completion of our bargain.'

'Our parent's bargain,' replied Raschida.

Marunesh spread his arms wide in supplication.

'Yet still I wait,' he said.

Raschida moved closer until she was almost within his grasp. The slender fingers of her free hand trimmed the sewn edges of her sari with an exaggerated grace and fluidity of movement until they seemed almost to dance along the cloth.

She straightened as Marunesh reached for her.

'What about your wife?' she asked, her eyes narrowed and quizzical.

'She is of no moment,' said Marunesh quickly, as his fingers met in fresh air.

'She is, as of this moment, your wife,' said Raschida.

'She is cold,' said Marunesh, 'I need a hearth such as yours by which I can sit in the winter of my life. I need feet to warm my back in the night.'

Raschida smiled seductively.

'And your other wives?'

Marunesh dismissed them with a negligent wave of his hand.

'I need a woman of fire,' he replied, 'Your heat would drive me to heights of passion such as are seen only in the carvings of the ancient temples.'

She looked him up and down again, then frowned.

'But where would I find you under all this fat?'

She moved an inch closer and prodded his belly with the handle of the whip. He was huge but hard and unyielding.

'Is there a man inside there?' she asked, 'Would I find the answer to our promise within?'

She prodded him again, 'And how many lives would I waste trying to find out?'

Marunesh eased himself clumsily out of the chair and staggered one or two steps towards her across the jetty.

'All is not what it may seem,' he said.

His hands rummaged beneath his voluminous robes. Raschida heard the soft whistle of leather sliding over leather and the distant click of withdrawn buckles. Marunesh himself seemed to lift upwards by inches as a large padded body harness slid out from beneath the robe and onto the jetty by his feet.

The robe sagged against him like a deflated tent and clung to the sweat of a body at least six stones lighter. He seemed to reach up and tower above her.

For the first time, Raschida felt the small insistent tingle of fear. Fear that her control of the situation was not as it had first seemed. Marunesh moved towards her, still huge, but now lighter of movement, graceful almost, and somehow, threatening.

She put up a hand and stopped him.

'And what shall be my Dowry?' she asked, 'By what price shall you secure the breaking of my promise to my husband?'

'You shall have your weight in gold,' said Marunesh. He reached out to touch her shoulder. She stepped back an inch. His fingers held in mid-air, empty.

'We will never have to return,' he said, 'There are other small plantations where we will be welcome and no one will know of this.'

He smiled down at her.

'You will never have to see the sadness of his face again.'

'When shall I have the gold?' asked Raschida.

'A little now. A little later,' said Marunesh, '...until I have paid you in full. And in that time we shall enjoy the finding and making of that gold from such unwary fools as your husband.'

'But I require my Dowry now,' said Raschida, '...for a woman does not feel that her commitment to a man can be consummated until the bargain of her purchase is wholly complete.'

'You realise,' said Marunesh, '...that this is against the tradition. But this is in itself an unusual transaction, that of breaking one promise in order to complete another, and as such, calls for an adjustment to the recognised measures.'

'I am sorry,' replied Raschida, '...but unless I feel that the bargain is complete, then I cannot be honest with you or with myself. And a lack of honesty is the one thing that will surely dampen my fire.'

Marunesh raised his hands into the air.

'Then I do not know,' he said, 'For your fire is what I need the most.'

'I am flattered,' said Raschida, feeling the timber firm again beneath her feet, '...by your promise of Dowry. But I am no longer new.'

'I do not care,' said Marunesh quickly.

'But I do,' said Raschida, 'I think that used goods, whilst there is still a certain honesty about them, and...' she paused and examined purposefully the smooth skin of her dark, slender fingers, stroked the soft silkiness of the inside of her exposed wrists, '...whilst they appear to have suffered little or no damage, may retain a slightly lesser value.'

'If that value could be placed, and found,' said Marunesh, '...then would the bargain be considered complete?'

'Shall we say,' replied Raschida, '...that it would clear a path and set out the terms by which I could consider such a request.'

Marunesh smiled in anticipation.

'Then what is your price?'

Raschida slid around him and sat herself deep into the vast brass chair, lost against the huge balances and chains.

'To weigh my bananas against my bodyweight, at ten rupees,' she said.

Marunesh rummaged through the coins in his purse, his lips working feverishly as he counted blind without removing his hands from the cloth.

'Alright,' he said. He looked around the dock.

'But who shall load them?'

'You can always leave them on the cart,' said Raschida.

Marunesh staggered across the jetty under the weight of the first bunch and dropped it onto the brass pan. Raschida shot up in the air, her face aglow with delight.

'That is not enough, in my opinion,' said Marunesh.

'Then let us consider opinions,' said Raschida, 'While I am given time to ponder, I am beginning to form an opinion as to your ripeness and condition. It may be that you have been on the tree too long.'

She indicated the discrepancy between the height of the pan and the base of the chair with her hand.

'Life is the balance of two weights,' she said, 'Greed and Vanity. If you assuage one, you anger the other, and I have not yet achieved the point of balance. I think you must take some from the bunch.'

Marunesh removed several large hands from the bunch until Raschida descended gracefully to hover at the mid-point of balance.

'That will be ten rupees,' she said, taking the coins from Marunesh and setting them down on the floor beside her dangling feet.

'Next bunch, please.'

The pile of coins grew until the cart was emptied and the boat was full and tipping its gunwales close to the water.

Raschida picked up the coins, counted out loud the ninety rupees and dropped them into the rough leather purse strung over her shoulder. Marunesh leaned against the scales. His robe clung to him and his face ran with perspiration. He undid a small button at the neck and sat down in the brass chair, panting like a summer dog.

'And what of our bargain?' He choked on a breath, 'Will you now join me on the boat of my life, forever?'

Raschida stepped onto the bulk of the body harness where it still lay on the jetty, pulled herself up into the cart and flicked the whip to wake the patient oxen. She glanced briefly at the discarded harness, then once more at the perspiration still soaking Marunesh's face.

'I might have,' she replied, '…but from what little I know of inflation, I think the wind has gone out of your sails.'

Titles in the CYBERMOUSE BOOKS range>

Our books are carefully selected, edited and published to bring you the finest reading experience whether on Kindle or in paperback.

'The Fox & The Fish' by Bill Allerton, ISBN: 978-0-9548373-2-7

Beset from all sides by Lovers, Coffins, Friends and Tinkers, Julius McEarly is forced to confront the greatest enemy of them all… his past. Set in Ireland, The Fox & The Fish carries a gentle but adult humour in a winsome, engaging storyline interspersed by moments of supremely funny 'codology'.

'We're in Ireland, and never far at all from the likes of Flann O'Brien, Joyce, Milligan, etc.. Casually very clever, so puzzling and allusive and fast that it makes the world more interesting when you stop. It gave me weird dreams; it is a weird dream.'
Rony Robinson (Author, Playwright and Sony Award winning BBC Radio presenter)

'Firelight on Dark Water' by Bill Allerton ISBN: 978-0-9930424-4-7
All of Life is in here. Seasons, Change, Wishes, Cookery, Sex, Death and Obsession, Guns, Trees and Bananas… even second hand Japanese brake parts…

'If you wish to be surprised and delighted by the change of direction presented in each story, then this is the book for you…'

'A Day for Tigers' by Bill Allerton ISBN: 978-0-9930424-3-0

A life-long love affair with Sci-Fi and Fantasy comics led to the collection of Bill Allerton's short SF stories into this 'Weird and Wonderful' edition.

In this book I have tried to recreate the sense of discovery that I felt when I first encountered SF, so… if like me you are still seven at heart, and also, like me, you are still in love with the Golden Age of Science Fiction and Fantasy, that you find that heart again within these pages.

'Warrior Girl' by Pauline Chandler ISBN: 978-0-9930424-0-9

Suppose, for just one moment, that your best friend has embarked on a path of faith and self-belief that will lead you into murder, intrigue, bloodshed and battles in which your own hands will not remain clean... Where would you stand? And when she is condemned to an unimaginably painful death?.. Where would you then stand? Beside her?

Warrior Girl is a heart-stopping retelling of the legend of St. Joan of Arc. Written from the point of view of Joan's cousin, Mariane De Courcey, the story convinces the reader that men aren't the only brave soldiers out there. Their combined story becomes one of betrayal, bravery, passion and battle.

'The healing revelation with which this novel ends is so unexpected and utterly right that it made me gulp.' Kevin Crossley-Holland, (The Guardian)

'The Jewellers Skin' by Ruth Valentine ISBN: 978-0-9548373-4-1

1946… England is recovering from war and change is upon everything. Nadia Humphreys is resident Cook at Holywell, a Victorian asylum on the outskirts of London, but now her past is coming to light, threatening not only her livelihood but also her hard-won sanity. Reaching from Kosovo to London and told with great insight and humour in vivid, luminous prose, The Jewellers Skin is an incredibly powerful Debut Novel from Ruth Valentine.

'The Ophelia Box' by Jenny Rodwell ISBN: 978-0-9930424-1-6

Beautifully crafted, this Debut Novel by Derbyshire based author Jenny Rodwell intrigues from the first lines. Her wonderfully dysfunctional characters are immediately recognisable and painted with such clarity that by the end of the first chapter we begin to wonder if we are not all somehow related…

Entered by Cybermouse Books for The Costa First Novel Awards 2015

'The Ophelia Box is written with an ingenious wit that made me smile long after I closed the lid…'
Bryony Doran, (Author of 'The China Bird' and 'The Sand Eggs')

'11 o'clock Chocolate Cake' by Caroline Pitcher
ISBN: 978-0-9548373-5-8

This book is an important part of the library of ANY pre-teen/early teen girl. Discover the joys and anxieties of turning sixteen even before you get there! Find the location of 'The Most Important Bus Stop At The Very Centre Of The Universe!' (*And make all of the six wonderful recipes in the book along the way…*)

'This is the story of a Summer just gone. It's the story of Lizzie and Star and Me, of Dodo, Pram Gran, Bottom Bob and Boss Woman, Tuba Boy… and the Beautiful Stranger… Who's telling this story? ME! Emma Peek.
Life changed for us all this Summer.'

'A Day for Tigers' by Bill Allerton
ISBN

Tales of The Weird and Wonderful
A Science Fiction Short Story Collection

…it's 1955 and you've just moved home. You go to the local newspaper shop for your Beano and find that they have a rack filled with 'Astounding Science Fiction', 'Weird Fantasy', 'Wonder Stories', 'Mandrake the Magician', with the occasional 'Green Lantern'. To top it all, they have 'The Eagle', with its truly sensational drawings by Frank Hampson illustrating the stories of 'Dan Dare, Pilot of the Future'.

I found within the pages of these magazines that Life Has No Boundaries. I've always suspected that our boundaries are self-set, and these 'pulps' as they were known, set my imagination free and on fire with all kinds of possibilities.

Sci-Fi, I Love You. There. I've said it. And now there's no going back.

In this book I have tried to recreate something of the sense of discovery that I felt when I first encountered this kind of story so, if, like me, you are still seven at heart, and also, like me, fell in love with the grand and the not-so-grand of Sci-Fi and Fantasy, then I hope you'll find your heart again within these pages.

Bill.

'Watch & Wait… *A Timeless Anthology***'** ISBN: 978-0-9548373-1-0

A collection of superb short works dedicated to 'Andrew', and all others living with Lymphoma.

Twenty authors… household names or major prize winners alongside others who soon will be… have gifted their short stories freely to this outstanding collection. The stories are eclectic, strangely familiar, or great and good fun. They will question your perception and challenge your accepted view of life and literature.

'Requiem' by Berlie Doherty   ISBN: 978-0-9548373-9-6

Set in both Ireland and Venice, Requiem follows the life and career of Opera star Cecelia Deardon. Probing the tragi-comedy of an Irish convent upbringing with a rare power and sensitivity, Requiem continues to disturb the reader long after the book is finished.

'I have great feelings of admiration for Requiem. This is a very good book indeed' Beryl Bainbridge

'Mine' by Caroline Pitcher ISBN: 978-0-9548373-8-9

Left alone in the Derbyshire cottage she has moved into with her mother, step-father and annoying brother, Shelley hears ancient and troubled voices, echoes from another time held within the thick stone walls for hundreds of years and now reaching out to her... Can Shelley help them find peace and, through that, can they help her to find her *own* identity?
'It's not MINE...' she says, *'Nothing is...'*

Written for the early teenage 'outsider', 'Mine' places the search for identity into several historical contexts, showing how only *some* things change through time.

'Vivid, beautifully written, I couldn't put it down...' Nicola Ho

Our books are available from all good bookshops, from Amazon and Amazon for Kindle, or direct from ourselves at;
http://www.cybermouse-multimedia.com

www.ingramcontent.com/pod-product-compliance
Lightning Source LLC
Chambersburg PA
CBHW060952120726
47910CB00002B/601